Turn To Me: An Erotic Romance
by Harley Easton

Prologue

"Big plans tonight, Chrissy?"

"Sure Mel," the brunette responded, locking up the last of her files in the drawer so they could be re-sorted and archived the following morning.

"Meaning you're stopping by the gym then getting yourself takeout," Mel prodded, grabbing his keys and cell phone off the desk. When Chrissy just smiled, he sighed. "Come to the house, Lorcan. Mimi has been bugging me about getting you over to see her for weeks. She's promised *arroz con pollo* if I can convince you."

Miguel Valintino, a.k.a. Mel, patted his slightly chubby belly. Chrissy's supervisor and ten years her senior, the adorable man was the perfect Hispanic husband and gentleman. He worked hard and expected a lot from everyone, but had also taken Chrissy under his wing when she'd moved to Florida in January. She'd practically become family. His wife, Mimi, was now one of her best friends and their kids, Dolce and Carlos, had taken to calling her Auntie. With how far she was from her own family, it was comforting to have a surrogate one.

"No can do, Mel." Chrissy picked up her bag and followed him out of Records. "I've got a date tonight."

Chrissy waved to the guys arriving for duty as she and Mel made their way out to the Polk County Police Department's parking lot. A bead of sweat dripped down the back of her neck. It was late, but the humidity was still too oppressive for the Michigan native. At least the warm September weather was better than what she'd experienced in July. Chrissy wondered if she'd ever get used to the new climate.

"You wouldn't lie to me now, would you, *pequeña*?" Mel raised an eyebrow. "Nobody from the force is dumb enough to hit on you."

It was true. As a records clerk, Chrissy wasn't required to do regular police training, yet still she had agreed to spar with the first overly aggressive sergeant to make an unwelcome pass at her. When her five-foot-five frame very publicly knocked his athletic six-foot ass to the floor hard enough to give him trouble breathing, she'd suddenly become a person of non-interest at the station. Dad taught her to handle alpha males well.

"Nope. Actually, Christoff shipped some Riesling from his vineyard in Germany, and it's been chilling in my fridge since last night. I'm going to uncork it and call my parents to toast their anniversary."

A few hours later, Chrissy took another sip of wine and savored it. Her cousin put this in storage a decade earlier when Chrissy had turned twenty-one. She'd wanted to drink it then but Christoff had pitched a fit, insisting that a proper German Riesling needed a decade to express its subtle flavors.

"If you're going to rush this," he'd chastised, shaking the bottle in her face. "I might as well serve you vinegar."

Owning a vineyard had made her cousin an insufferable wine snob, but he knew what he was doing. The sweet, floral potable he shipped her twice a year had ruined her for all other white wines. Luckily, Christoff sent the bottles a crate at a time.

Chrissy smiled at the white wolf label as she poured herself another glass and settled down on the couch. As an ongoing reminder that he knew best, Christoff only pressed this particular wine for her and dressed it with a speciality mark. She momentarily wondered if her parents had received the bottle she'd had Christoff send for their anniversary dinner.

Taking a sip, she glanced at the clock. Almost nine. They must really be celebrating. When Chrissy called at 6:00 p.m. as prearranged, her parents had just arrived at the restaurant. Dad had driven Mom to some new place in Marquette, and she was too excited to talk at the time. Mom promised to call after dinner.

Chrissy was beginning to get worried, however, when the phone rang. Catching the area code on the Caller ID, she snatched it.

"Hey Mom! You're late. Did you have a nice dinner?" "Babygirl?"

It wasn't her mother.

"Joseph?" Joseph Engel was the grandson of a longtime family friend. The boy could have been an international model, and he'd been recruited a couple of times, but instead chose to stay at his family's small store in the Upper Peninsula. He was the closest thing Chrissy had to a younger brother. Usually he was all laughs but something in his tone wasn't right. Fear clenched her stomach. "Joseph, what's wrong?"

"Chrissy, baby. I need you to go pack yourself a bag. I've called Mel and Mimi to have them drive you to the airport." His voice was very calm and smooth. It was the same tone Chrissy had heard detectives at the station use countless times. "I've booked you a red-eye into Detroit and the earliest connection I could into Escanaba. I'll be there to pick you up at one tomorrow when you land."

"Joseph, what happened?" Chrissy heard a key click the lock of her front door. Without a word, Mimi walked into her bedroom. Mel sat down on the couch and put a hand on her knee.

"It's your mom and dad," Joseph said, gravely. Chrissy's hand shook as she registered the pause before his voice softened. "There's been an accident."

Sixteen Months Later

The lakefront property had been in Chrissy's family for several generations. When the Torstens first came to the Upper Peninsula in the early 1800s, there were hardly any cities established. They'd built a small cabin and stayed, remaining when the miners and loggers began to inhabit the area and lasting through the establishment of government regulated forests.

Grandpa Torsten gave the property to Chrissy's mother when she became a Lorcan. The memories of summers nestled in the mountains, forests, and lakes with Mom, Dad, and Grandpa Torsten were some of Chrissy's best. Now simply looking at the house she loved brought tears to her eyes.

Dad and Grandpa Torsten built the lake house together when Chrissy was about six. Secluded as it was, the cabin had become a popular vacation spot for city families. The lake was fed by a hot spring that made it perfect for summer swimming, and the snowmobiling was great in the winter.

The additional income had allowed her parents retire a bit early. Chrissy sniffed, brushing at the tears forming in her eyes. They were supposed to be able to enjoy their retirement for much longer than they actually had.

When Chrissy had decided to move, her dad extracted a promise that she would visit them during the summers. She didn't have time off the first year at Polk County, but he said he understood. She'd never get the opportunity to keep her promise now.

The car accident happened almost two years ago, but it'd taken nearly fourteen months for Chrissy to come to terms with the loss, and decide to return to Michigan. She'd made sure to come back in January. Returning in the summer would remind her too much of her absent family.

Despite the overwhelming emotions regarding the property, Chrissy hadn't wanted to give the place up. Instead, she'd hired a company to keep it open for rentals. In the end, Mimi convinced her that she would never deal with her ghosts while living in Florida. Now back home, Chrissy planned to use the more rustic cabin in the woods when she wanted to escape. The lake house tenants would never know she was there.

She took one last look at the place and began the ninety-minute drive back to Marquette. Chrissy hadn't been willing to make the trek out to the lake house until she'd re-established herself. There were simply too many memories. Instead she'd spent a week unpacking her new apartment—which Joseph's grandma, Mama Engel, had insisted on helping with—and another week getting used to her new job.

Escanaba would have been closer but Marquette PD was the only station that had an opening for a property clerk. As she made it out from the access road to the highway, Chrissy let her thoughts drift to work.

Her coworkers seemed all right. The Records supervisor, Keith Cavanaugh, was a short, gruff, old Irishman with a foul-mouth. But she was pretty sure she'd won him over with the homemade butterscotch cookies and fifth of whiskey she'd brought as thank you for showing her the ropes that week. He'd made certain to take her around the departments, and she'd been asked out to drinks on Tuesday with a few girls from Traffic. The only negative response she'd gotten was in Homicide.

Cavanaugh had introduced her to a team: a short redheaded woman with a warm smile and a curly-headed blond man with the longest legs Chrissy had ever seen. The guy bordered on roguishly handsome with his high cheekbones and arrestingly blue eyes, but killed it the moment he spoke.

"God," he huffed. "Don't tell me we have to train *another* one, Cavanaugh." His hand gestured at Chrissy as if she was a child he'd been stuck babysitting.

"Wouldn't have to keep bringing in new clerks if one particular asshole in Homicide would stop scaring them off." The Irishman punctuated his statement with a firm jab to the blond's shoulder, making him wince and rub the spot in annoyance. "Now shut the fuck up, Sutherlund, before you chase this one off too. She's a fine-looking woman, and I ain't so far in the grave that I can't appreciate a bit of sunshine."

"Christina Lorcan," she'd stated, reaching out a hand toward the disgruntled detective in an attempt to salvage the situation. "I'm a quick study, promise."

Sutherlund had crossed his arms and stared at her. His partner took Chrissy's hand instead, offering her a smile. "Bridgette Bergin," she'd interjected warmly. "Ignore Landen. He's not always a grumpy bastard. We're glad to have you."

They'd chatted amicably for a few minutes, but Landen hadn't spoken another word. His stance remained tense and his eyes distressed. By the time Cavanaugh declared the detective an "inconsiderate cock" and a "right sorry waste of God's gift of life," sweat had broken out beneath Landen's beautiful curls. Chrissy had wondered if he was sick or if she'd really upset him so easily.

Even now, months later, she couldn't figure out why he'd had such a strange reaction.

Chrissy decided it didn't matter. She turned on the radio and made a left turn onto Highway 69. She'd loop through Escanaba on the way to Marquette. It would take her an extra half-hour to get home taking that route instead of 95, but it was more than worth it not to have to pass the crash site. She had good memories of the cabin to buffer the loss, but none along that terrible stretch of road. Going that route, she might decide to drive off and join her mom and dad.

Chapter One

"Sutherlund, what's got your panties in a knot?" Bergin asked, dropping to sit on his desk. "You keep it up like that in meetings and Captain Goring will have you on desk duty for the next month. Try to calm down a bit, all right?"

Chrissy watched from the doorway for several minutes as Bridgette attempted to calm down her usually wisecracking partner. Anyone could tell it wasn't working. After a few minutes Bergin gave up, offering Sutherlund a pat on the back before leaving. As soon as she was out of sight, the detective dropped his head to the desk.

Chrissy found her infatuation with the detective a little disconcerting. Things had started off on the wrong foot, but it wasn't that. It was obvious to Chrissy that they shared similar backgrounds so after the initial meeting, she decided the best approach was simply to wear him down with kindness. It had sort of worked. He was still evasive but no longer hostile. She'd even coaxed a smile out of him every now and then. Still there was something about Landen that made her uncharacteristically unsure of herself.

When the tag came in to deliver cold case boxes to Homicide, Chrissy grabbed and fulfilled the request herself, hoping to catch a glimpse of her favorite brooding detective. Unfortunately her typical bad timing with Sutherlund was in full force, and she'd walked in just in time to hear Goring slam the door and witness the scene between Landen and his partner. Not wanting him to know she saw, Chrissy turned to take the boxes back downstairs.

"What?" he barked at her back, causing her to flinch. Landen's sharp hearing must have caught the click of her heels on the linoleum.

Blushing, Chrissy turned to face him. "I, um..." She lifted the case boxes in her hand by way of explanation. "Files for the Lindholm and Asher investigations."

She couldn't blame Sutherlund for his tone. The poor man truly looked like he'd been having a day from hell. Landen shook his head sheepishly and muttered something under his breath. Chrissy's heart skipped as she watched his hand rake distractedly through his mess of flaxen hair, a nervous habit she found particularly endearing. As he checked the clock, she noted that his ordinarily clear, azure eyes were flecked with worry and amber hues.

In the six months since she'd transferred to the Records department in Marquette, Chrissy had been carefully studying Landen. Luckily anyone who had noticed her attentive nature had brushed it off as an infatuation with the charming detective. It wasn't as if she was the only one with that problem.

Yes, she had to admit that the button- down shirts he preferred always showed just the right amount of chest hair, and his runner's ass looked perfectly grabbable in the low-slung jeans he got away with wearing despite dress code. But she'd also made careful note of how his mess of curls appeared longer at certain times, and how his eyes gained golden flecks whenever he was upset. Chrissy's instincts alerted her to his nature the day they met, but his abrupt attitude had kept her at arm's length. After watching him closely for months, she had finally come to a conclusion as to why Landen was so unusually standoffish with her.

Chrissy knew she had to say something today. She'd put it off long enough. Setting the boxes on the desk, she reached over and placed a hand on his shoulder. The touch was meant to be reassuring but, as always, Landen tensed under her fingers.

She withdrew, assessing him with concern. "Is everything okay?"

"Yeah," he exhaled, putting on a fake smile and tapping his extremely fidgety fingers on
the desk. "Sorry I snapped at you. Bridge is right. I'm just on edge."

"Well, you could make it up to me," she hinted, casually flipping the chestnut braid off her shoulder.

Landen crinkled his forehead and eyed her curiously. Chrissy couldn't tell him that she'd been thinking about doing this for months, that she had noticed how his eyes followed her
whenever she delivered files from Records. It was obvious to anyone looking that he was aware of her, but he stubbornly kept his distance. Now Chrissy decided, it was time for a push.

"Drinks after work?" she suggested. "It'll help that headache."

"How did you know —" he began then dropped it. Gold slashed through his eyes for a split second. When he blinked, they slipped back to cool-blue pools. His nostrils flared slightly, unnoticeable to anyone who wasn't deliberately looking for the response. A deep sigh escaped Landen's lips. "Thanks. I'll pass." His anxious eyes flicked once more to the clock on the wall as his phone rang.

She saw it was only his buddy Mark from Traffic. Chrissy placed her hand over the receiver, enjoying the surprised look on Landen's face. "So you're not really that sorry?" She goaded him with a smile.

His forehead crinkled in response. "No," he sputtered. "I mean, yes. Really Chrissy, it's just I'm leaving after work for a few days away. I was planning on heading out right after my shift. Mark was probably calling about watching my house this weekend. I should call him back."

"Sure." She knew his excuse was just a defense mechanism to keep people from getting too close. Dropping her gaze she lifted her hand from the receiver. Landen reached out but grabbed for the phone instead of her hand.

"And office relations policy and all," he continued, dialing. His tone was casual, but those eyes she loved were sad. "You should just stay away from me."

"I understand. No drinks after work."

Landen's whole body sagged. Chrissy couldn't tell if he was relieved or disappointed that she'd given up so easily.

"We'll just have to have one at the lake," Chrissy said brightly as she walked away.

She was outside the glass doors of the department before this registered in his tired brain. Behind her she heard the detective yell, "Wait. What?!" Smiling, she headed back down the stairs to Records.

Chapter Two

Chrissy had known Landen was renting out the lake house every month for quite a while. She recognized him in the reservation office once when she was signing some paperwork, but he was completely unaware he'd been escaping to her place. However, it took a few months before she realized her visits always coincided with Landen's. The joy of the rentals being run through a second party was that Chrissy never needed to know the details of the people staying in the house. It was better that way.

Landen was different. When she started seeing him more often at work, and started noticing details — like the agitation that became depression when the flecks filled eyes or the increased tension in his jaw as those blond spirals got shaggier, even the way he inhaled sharply whenever she dropped off files — that's when Chrissy requested the renters' logs and noticed their visits were always the same time. Since then she'd kept an eye on him. He was invariably alone and never left the lake house during his stay. Given what she knew about him, she began checking the cabin after his stays.

Landen was the only tenant Chrissy didn't hire the cleaning service to pick up after. She knew it was odd, but she wanted to know more about the quiet detective. However, he gave her painfully little to work with. The lake house rarely looked used when he drove back to the city. Landen took out the small amount of trash he created and never left dishes in the sink. The only clear sign of his presence was the set of sheets in the laundry sack. They smelled so strongly of him that Chrissy almost couldn't bear to wash them.

It saddened her how closed off Detective Sutherlund was. Every once in a while there would be a flash of something more. He'd let loose a snip of biting sarcasm in the middle of the office, or sit tapping his long fingers on the rim of his morning coffee and seem serenely peaceful for a few seconds.

Chrissy knew she glimpsed the real Landen in those moments before his jawline hardened and his eyes regained their troubles. It was obvious he was guarding himself. She could help if he would only let her close enough. After his outburst today, she couldn't wait any longer.

She pulled onto the property around seven and walked up to the door. A savory aroma wafted out from the open windows, and Chrissy smiled as Landen's off-key voice warbled along with Sinatra. The bachelor knew how to cook and apparently he cooked to music.

There was something comforting about the relaxed nature of the scene she imagined going on in the kitchen. Chrissy would have loved to sit on the wraparound porch and listen to him all night, but that wouldn't solve anyone's problems. Taking a deep breath, she knocked on the door.

"Shit!" The expletive was accompanied by a loud bang and a series of scuffling noises. Chrissy's teeth gripped her bottom lip. Again, her timing with the detective was anything

but perfect. She waited patiently as a series of thundering footsteps came toward her.

"Who the hell—" he began, ripping back the door. Landen's mouth snapped shut when he saw who was standing at the step. His whole body language shifted from angry to anxious.

"Hi, Landen," Chrissy managed to squeak out. It wasn't his attitude that had her unnerved, it was his appearance.

Detective Sutherlund had answered the door clad only in jeans that displayed a small trail of pale curls dipping beneath the waistband. His heaving shoulders and chiseled abs were incredibly distracting as was the flash of his eyes when they swept over her tight jeans and leather jacket.

"What are you doing here?"

Chrissy watched as he tried to regain his composure by leaning against the door, gripping his hand around the frame, and taking a deep breath. If he was trying to appear comfortable, it wasn't working. His body was still rigid with tension. She couldn't really blame him; he came up here to avoid company.

"I told you we'd have drinks at the lake," Chrissy said with a smile, offering the half-dressed detective the bottle of wine she'd brought with her. He just stared at it.

"I told you we really shouldn't see each other," Landen reminded her, but Chrissy was undeterred.

"Because of the office policy, I know, but I'm here on official business. I thought I should meet my most frequent renter. Consider this a thank you from the landlord instead of a drink between coworkers." Trying a lighthearted approach, she offered him a wink.

Luckily it disarmed the detective enough to make him take the wine. "Kleiner Geisterwolf," he read from the bottle, and then eyed her curiously. "Little Ghost Wolf?"

"A family joke," Chrissy explained, shrugging her shoulders. "The wine is from my cousin's vineyard in Germany, and he only makes this particular type for me. Ghost Wolf is my signature label. You are extremely lucky; I don't share it with many people. So," she glanced behind him, into the house, "are you going to invite me in, or keep me on the porch?"

"Now's really not a good time." Landen's voice was uncertain and his eyes carried those gold flecks again.

For a minute, Chrissy worried she'd misjudged the situation. She folded her arms protectively around herself and kicked at the boards of the deck with her boot. "Oh, do you have someone with you?"

"No!" His response came a little too quick, making Chrissy's heart jump.

She couldn't resist harassing him a little bit. "So, you answer the door half-naked, find a woman offering you a bottle of wine, and you're not going to invite her in to what is technically her own house?"

Landen glanced down at his chest as if suddenly realizing he was shirtless. Ruffling his blond locks, he muttered something in frustration. "Yes. No. I..."

She took advantage of his confusion, pushing by the detective to head toward the kitchen. "I'll grab a couple of glasses," Chrissy called lightly. "Don't worry. I know where they're at."

"Fuck," she heard him say to himself.

From the corner of her eye, Chrissy saw his shoulders sag as he shut the door. It would have disappointed her if she hadn't reached the kitchen by that point and been startled at the complete disarray.

It instantly became obvious that Landen was shirtless because he'd tipped an entire pan's worth of his dinner down his front. The still steaming dish was in the sink and his shirt was lying on the floor along with what looked like some sort of vegetable mix. Shards of glass also peppered the scene. The floor was sticky with spilled beer.

Without a word, Chrissy grabbed a broom from the closet. It was only fair to help clean up since she'd caused the mess. When Landen finally padded in quietly, she was bending over the glass. Chrissy swore she heard a hitch in his breath and a small surge of joy ran through her body knowing she caused the reaction.

First and foremost Chrissy was here to help him, but she wouldn't be opposed to attracting his attention. She was so focused on the happy notion that she nearly missed him reaching for the dustpan.

"Uh-uh. Barefoot," Chrissy said, pointing in the general direction of his long legs. "Glass. I'll get it cleaned up."

She made quick work of mopping up the mess in the kitchen, while Landen stayed on the other side of the breakfast bar. Chrissy was conscious of him watching her the entire time. When she finally stood up, his eyes caught hers.

A brief nod was all it took for him to glide into the kitchen. With one long arm, he reached around her and grabbed two dinner plates from the cabinet, effectively pinning her between the counter and his warm body.

"Stay for dinner," he demanded, his hips pressing into hers. The contact made Chrissy breathless and her cheeks flushed. Landen pulled away and became overly careful again. Walking to the oven, he removed the remains of his dinner.

"You'll need to leave right after," he grunted. It stung a little, but Chrissy's feelings were eased at the flustered look on the detective's face. His eyes drifted closed and his forehead creased in worry before he added, "I want to make sure you get home safe."

"It's sweet of you to be so protective, Landen, but I grew up around here," Chrissy said, pulling a corkscrew out of the drawer and opening the wine with a satisfyingly audible pop. "Nothing in these woods is going to harm me."

"You don't know that." His tone was as tight as the line of his lips as he accented the statement by slamming the oven door.

Deciding it was time to stop dancing around the topic, Chrissy poured herself a glass and downed half of it. Then she refilled it and set it down with a clink that made Landen turn. She could tell he wasn't prepared to find her in front of him, pressing a single finger directly into his chest.

"Nothing is going to hurt me, Landen. Nothing. That includes you, so stop treating me like I'm breakable and actually listen to me for thirty seconds."

His eyes widened at her unexpected forcefulness. "You don't—"

"Yes, actually I do," she cut him off. "It's exactly two hours and twenty-three minutes until sundown and moonrise is maybe ten minutes after. You got some time, so why don't you tell me how long you've had lycanthropy."

Chapter Three

There. She finally said it. For a second the tension in the room was almost tangible, but then it shattered as Landen wrapped those long fingers around her head, drawing her in close. He pressed his nose to her scalp, inhaling her fragrance like he'd been drowning and she was he only oxygen left in the room.

"It's not possible," he said, retreating and staring at her in awe. "Your scent. You don't smell like — "

"I'm a Skip." Chrissy turned away from the kitchen and walked into the living room, stopping only long enough to pick up the glasses and the wine from the breakfast bar. She figured it'd be best if Landen was seated for this conversation.

Apparently he had the same idea as he dropped into a chair, stretched out his legs, and began playing with the curls at his temples. "A *Skip*?" he whispered.

Taking a seat on the arm of the chair, Chrissy passed over one of the wine glasses. Landen stared at her, barely seeming to register the glass in his hands. "Yep. Gotta love genetics. Both Mom and Dad were full Weres. I got everything but the shape-shifting."

He gazed up at her with wide, blue eyes. Chrissy tried not to think how many times she had wished to be exactly what he was struggling not to be. She ached to pull those curls close to her chest,
listen to him breathing while she explained the joy that could come from shifting. But now was not the time to overwhelm him with details. Landen needed time to process that he wasn't alone.

"So you know..." He hesitated.

Chrissy decided to continue for him. "How sometimes you can hear a pen scratching two rooms away? How super-healing sounds like a great thing until it burns like hellfire in your veins? How the moon sings in your blood on nights like this and all you want to do is eat, and hunt, and…" Chrissy trailed off, taking a sip of wine. She was not drunk enough to mention how lycanthropy heightened arousal, but she was pretty sure Landen sensed her unspoken words.

"And you're not scared?"

She looked down to see his finger tracing the seam of her jeans. "Of you?" Chrissy bit back a laugh. "Landen, you're too worried. I've been around wolves my whole life. I can't even date humans anymore. It takes a wolf to—"

Chrissy didn't get a chance to finish the statement. Landen lunged, and she found herself falling backward off the chair. He caught her in his arms, his lips pressing fiercely to hers. Both glasses clattered to the floor as he held her close, firmly supporting her back with one hand while the other fought with the button on her jeans. A deep growl rumbled in his throat as Chrissy stared into his now golden eyes.

She whimpered in response and grasped his shoulders. Landen gently lowered her to the floor before ripping the jeans from her body. After months of careful words and avoided situations, his impatience was thrilling. Chrissy reached for him, but his long fingers gripped her wrists and pressed them into the floor above her head. He straddled her, assessing his prey with an appreciative gaze.

Chrissy took a deep breath, letting Landen's scent fill her senses. He smelled woodsy and feral. She hadn't been with anyone since before her parent's accident, and Detective Sutherlund was definitely her type. Playfully, she rolled her hips against him, knowing that this close to sundown his instincts would take over. The contact earned her another growl as his tongue invaded her mouth.

She pressed into him, her need intense and her body insistent—though she was finding it hard to breathe. Breaking the kiss, Landen released her hands and began peeling off her shirt. Chrissy jerked as his teeth grazed over her bra, teasing her hard nipples as he worked his way down. She mewled appreciatively when they left a half-moon imprint on her hip. Heat pooled between her legs as he gripped the fabric covering her and jerked harshly, tearing off her panties.

Landen's tongue lapped teasingly against her clit. Those changed eyes regarded Chrissy carefully through her splayed legs. He inhaled deeply before rolling his tongue to rim the opening of her entrance. She moaned in anticipation as he thrust his tongue deep inside. Chrissy wound a hand in Landen's perfect curls while the other reached to entwine their fingers together. She cried out in pleasure. Fierce, but tender, was the wolf way.

As the desire coiled inside, a whimper escaped her throat. Pleasant as this was, it wasn't why Chrissy had followed him here. She longed for something so sweet with Landen, but tonight was about teaching him to handle the wolf. With significant effort, she pushed him away and rolled up to her knees. Chrissy could see his wildness and felt the tension surge through Landen's entire body.

"Mine," he snarled, reaching for her. He was too close to the transition to restrain his instincts.

Chrissy met him full on as any Alpha should. She bit across his collarbone as he wrapped his arms around her waist. He lifted her easily and tossed her onto the couch. As she righted herself, she heard the clink of a belt buckle and the tell- tale sounds of a zipper. Landen stood naked before her, his body completely mesmerizing. She couldn't resist running her nails along his hips and weaving her fingers through the trail of pale hair she'd admired earlier.

The detective stared down at her, his erect cock a clear indication of his enthusiasm. But he made no move. Recognizing the display of dominance, Chrissy pushed her hair out of the way and offered her neck.

That was all it took.

Instantly Landen was upon her, rolling her body beneath him so that she knelt on the couch with her front pressed into the firm cushions. He roughly pushed her legs further apart with his knee and drove into her from behind, completely filling her with the first stroke. Chrissy gasped when he pulled back, ramming into her again and again.

Landen's hands roamed her body, kneading and pinching her most sensitive places as he bit the back of her neck. Chrissy mewled. Each small dose of pain was accompanied with almost cruel jolts of pleasure. She spiraled higher and higher, his length hitting that sweet spot deep inside, causing her whole body to quiver.

"More," she begged, feeling his arms pull her closer. His body pressed into hers as he rocked. When he came it was the sweetest sensation yet, pushing her over into bliss. Drifting back to earth, she noticed Landen was still inside of her. He held her tight as he softened, running his tongue along the bite marks he'd left.

"Lan?" Chrissy questioned, reaching around to run a finger along his beautiful face. "I could really hurt you," he whispered in her ear, pulling his body away.

She could sense him wrestling with the warring personalities within him, the primal nature of the wolf at odds with the protective side that had certainly driven him to become a detective. Right now both sides of him were losing. It pained her to see him in such torment. That was the reason she was here.

Turning to face him, she placed her palm to his chest, feeling the pulse of his heart. "I told you before, nothing is going to hurt me, including you."

His eyes were still golden. It was getting too close to the change for him to trust her words. Sighing, Chrissy slipped from underneath him and moved back toward the kitchen.

"Where are you going?" he asked, worry filling his voice.

"To get you something to eat. The sex was amazing, but you're going to need your strength if we're running tonight."

Chapter Four

Luckily the fish on the stove was still pretty warm when Chrissy pulled off the lid. She scooped it onto the plates and shuffled through the fridge for a replacement for the vegetables. Finding little, she settled on cutting up some lettuce for a salad and made a mental note to head to the store tomorrow. Neither of them was going to get through the weekend if she didn't stabilize his diet. Hearing a noise behind her, Chrissy turned to find Landen staring at her in wonder.

"Dinner?" she asked, offering him the plate.

He took it silently and sat down at the table. Taking a bite, Landen chewed thoughtfully but continued to stare. Chrissy left him long enough to slip her jeans back on, sans ruined panties, and came back to the table.

"You're fucking a werewolf." The detective shook his head in disbelief, taking another bite off his plate.

"Nice vocabulary," Chrissy tossed back at him. "And I could point out that you just nailed your coworker and current landlord, so don't be so quick to judge."

Landen dropped his fork and glared at her. Chrissy stared back unwaveringly.

"I just attacked you," he continued, as if trying to convince her. When she smiled, his face turned sour. "We didn't even use protection."

"Our blood is a natural healing serum, Landen. No condom is safer than that. And I'm pretty sure it takes a doctor to dislodge my IUD."

"How can you possibly be okay with this?"

Something nagged at the back of her mind. Originally, Chrissy assumed the detective was merely hiding the fact he was a werewolf. But now he knew she was one, too, and yet he seemed skeptical. She wondered if there was more to it than feeling alone. Only one thing made sense to her.

"Oh, God. You're a Turn, aren't you?"

Landen flinched as if she'd spit on him. His eyes were suddenly glued to his plate. "I don't know what that means. Other than the obvious, what's wrong with me?"

"Absolutely nothing. I thought you were an untrained Were." Chrissy's hand reached out to cup Landen's, softening her voice to let him know she was sincere. "Being a Turn means you weren't born a wolf. It explains quite a bit, like why you're so worried all the time. You probably have a lot of questions." Chrissy paused, giving Landen a chance to ask whatever he needed. When he remained pensively quiet she gently asked. "How long since the accident?"

Landen took the hand lying over his and turned it. His thumb rubbed gently over the skin between her thumb and index finger. Chrissy was always amused by the way his fidgety fingers could never seem to stop moving.

"About eighteen months ago," he divulged. "Bridge and I picked up this strange one by the national forest preserve. Car off to the side of the road smashed to bits but the bodies inside didn't have a scratch. They were so clean, it looked like they'd been placed in the vehicle after it was wrecked, which was impossible because the car had rolled over two or three times. Looked like the thing went through a trash compactor."

Chrissy's chest tightened and her stomach clenched. It wasn't possible. Landen continued, unaware of the effect his words were having.

"So we're chatting with the ME and the female just convulses. No way she was even breathing by that point, but I swear she lunged forward. Scared the shit out of me and gave Bridge a good laugh. I didn't think much of it, but I get home and I've got what looks like some wicked claw marks down the back of my leg. Next I know, I'm a damn dog every month."

Chrissy exhaled and gently removed her hand. Noticing Landen hadn't really touched his food, she picked up a piece of fish and popped it in his mouth. Taking the hint, he grabbed his fork and started eating again.

"At least it was a scratch and not a bite. A bite might have killed you. The only reason you feel like a dog is because you're not taking care of yourself. Fish is fine, but red meat is better for you when you shift." Chrissy walked to the sink and flipped on the faucet, continuing the conversation as she started on the dishes. "We're going shopping tomorrow to get you some venison and whatever else I can talk the butcher into. The shop in Norway has a standing order for me. Tonight we'll go running, and then—"

"You mentioned that earlier," Landen interrupted. "What do you mean by 'running'?" *He can't be serious,* Chrissy thought. She turned off the water and faced Landen, bracing herself against the sink. "Running. In the woods. Letting the moon burn your skin and the wind fill your lungs. It's the best part of being a wolf. I'm stuck on two legs, but even I go running. What do you usually do when you wolf out?"

Instead of answering, Landen walked over to a duffel bag sitting on the kitchen floor and pulled out a couple of syringes and several bottles. He calmly punctured one of the vials with a needle and pulled the liquid into a syringe. "Time to take this now anyway," he muttered.

In an instant, Chrissy was next to him, knocking the syringe to the floor. He barely had time to register what had happened before she smacked him hard across the cheek. Landen's hand rose to his reddened face.

"You've been coming into my house and tranqing yourself every month?!" Chrissy was shaking. "What is wrong with you?"

"I won't hurt someone," he growled, challenging her authority.

Right now you're hurting yourself!" she yelled back. Chrissy rose to full height, still small, but unyielding against his six-two frame. She'd dealt with Alphas her entire life. Even if she couldn't shift, she wasn't about to back away from this fight. Landen's fists and jaw clenched as his body shook with tension. It was evident that he and his wolf were warring for control of the situation. Chrissy remained firm, knowing his wolf would recognize the subtle shift in her shoulders and the stern set of her eyes. She was an alpha female. This was a challenge he would lose.

"I understand that you haven't had the best introduction to being a wolf, but that is no excuse. I'll teach you," she continued. "You are in my house, covered in my scent. That means you are now part of my pack. I don't let people hurt members of my pack. Even, and especially, themselves."

Landen's head drooped, and Chrissy noticed his mass of soft curls. They were starting to get longer. It wouldn't be long before he shifted.

"What do you expect me to do?" Landen's voice was barely a whisper.

Tentatively she ran a hand through his hair and along his cheek. His hand cupped hers. When he lifted his head there was no blue left in those gorgeous eyes.

"I expect you to run with me."

Walking into the living room, Chrissy grabbed her bra and shoes. Summer runs were exhilarating; both because they were so short and the warmer weather allowed her to wear so little. Summer was the season she felt most like a true wolf. It was as close as she could get to freedom without shifting.

Landen remained naked. Clothes would only hinder him when he shifted. He seemed uneasy, but Chrissy had exerted enough dominance that he wouldn't question her for now. When she walked outside, he simply followed. Twilight fell as they neared the rocky area overlooking the lake.

She turned to face him. "Look, this whole side of the property is bordered by the lake. There are miles of woods until you hit the edge of the nearest property to the west. You drove up from the south so you know we're a good ways from town. And the north is all forest preserve. Tourist house. No neighbors. It's why my family kept the property. You can't hurt anyone out here."

Landen draped his arms around Chrissy's waist and nuzzled her neck. His warm breath sent a shiver up her spine and took her back to earlier that evening. Her libido ran high during the full moon and as much as she knew she shouldn't, all Chrissy wanted to do was tackle the sexy detective.

"I could hurt you," he worried again. Landen's whole body was twitching, his eyes almost glowing.

Chrissy could tell he was only minutes from shifting. She dropped to the ground, pulling him with her. As they lay on the grassy spot on the cliffs, she brought his head to her chest, whispering comforting words and brushing her fingers along the side of his head. The transition would be easier if she could calm his rapid breathing.

"Covered in my scent. Part of my pack. The wolf in you won't hurt me, and I won't let you hurt anyone else. I promise."

Landen exhaled and seconds later she felt his body contort atop hers. Pulling herself to her knees, Chrissy found herself gazing into Landen's golden eyes behind a long snout. The wolf shook his head, sniffing her experimentally.

She kept eye contact, extending her hand and threading it through the tawny pelt behind his ears. Landen grinned, his tongue lolling out of his mouth. As Chrissy stood, he brushed his head against her, batting at her legs with his tail to scent her body. Yes, the wolf accepted her as packmate and, apparently, lover. She hoped human Landen would be as understanding the next morning.

The wolf whined and pranced in anticipation. One look from Chrissy and they set off, chasing one another through the woods. She pumped her legs hard, willing herself to feel the sting of the air in her lungs and the moon singing in her marrow.

She was free. Landen was safe. Neither of them was alone any longer. Tonight it was all that mattered.

Chapter Five

When Chrissy awoke the next morning, sunlight was peeking though the room-darkening curtains. She tried to stretch her weary muscles but found her movement was restricted. She looked down and saw Landen wrapped around her body. A smile crossed her face. His legs were entwined with hers, his arms clutching at her shoulders, and his mess of curls was nestled to her breasts. Trying not to wake him, she ran her hand though his hair and traced the muscles down his back.

He ran last night, oh how he ran, chasing her as if nothing on earth were more important than keeping her in sight. The two of them kept going until her lungs burned for air and the moon dipped on the horizon. It was only then, exhausted, they walked back to the house. Landen shifted back moments before they reached the door.

She knew nothing happened — a wolf's first run was always overwhelmingly tiring — but it was somehow comforting to discover they had ended the evening together in bed. It was as if they had been made for each other and, in a way, they had. Chrissy dismissed the thought. She could think about those consequences later. For now, it was time to see if his human side was as comfortable with this as his wolf.

"Lan?" she whispered, loving that for the second time she'd gotten to use her pet name for him. He moved, holding her tighter in his sleep and breathing in deeply. It was a shame to wake him when he seemed so peaceful and content, but they had things to accomplish before he shifted again that evening.

"Lan," she stated more firmly. "Wake up."

His eyes fluttered open and a second later he inhaled sharply. Chrissy giggled, knowing that her pert nipple was his first sight of the morning. At the noise he bolted off the bed, staring at her.

"Shit!"

The smile dropped from her face. This was not how she'd hoped this would go. Uncomfortably, she grasped the sheet tight to her body, covering her naked flesh. Landen looked down at his own state of undress and cursed again, running an agitated hand across his face.

"Did I? Oh, God, tell me I didn't." He moved toward her, but Chrissy couldn't meet his eyes. Curling into a ball, she bit her lip as her brain tried to string together a sentence to calm the situation.

"I hurt you," he stated, crestfallen.

Chrissy's head shot up. After yesterday he was still worried about that? "No!" she cried out, shaking her head. "No."

From his hunched shoulders, Chrissy could tell that Landen didn't believe her. She dropped the sheet and crawled to the edge of the bed where he stood. As the fabric pooled on the floor, she caressed his body with her lips, kissing his forehead, his eyes, his lips — anything she could reach to comfort him. Gently, Landen pulled away in disbelief.

"See for yourself," Chrissy stated, jumping off the bed to pull back the drapes. The room flooded with light, revealing a breathtaking view of the cliffs and the lake edge they ran last night. In the sun it was easy to see her creamy flesh held no red marks. Landen gaped so she turned, offering him a full view.

"Not a scratch."

Landen's tongue darted out of his mouth, wetting his lips. His eyes were bluer than they had been the previous evening, but were still flecked with amber. The full moon was tonight. The wolf would be more present today than any other. Chrissy knew he wasn't sated. Having been allowed to run the previous evening, his wolf would expect freedom this morning.

Lust rolled off Landen in waves; the wolf's appetite was purely carnal. Chrissy's eyes glassed over and her knees went weak thinking about it. She tried to brace herself by grabbing the arm of the reading chair that graced the corner of the bedroom.

"Do you intend to stare at me like that all morning?" she asked.

Landen stalked toward her, the slant of his strong shoulders predatory and alluring. "And exactly how am I staring at you?"

"Like you're starving," Chrissy whispered, "and I'm breakfast."

He circled, roping her into his arms and running his tongue from her shoulder up to her ear. Grazing the tender lobe with his teeth, Landen groaned and pressed himself against her bare bottom. "But I am starving, dove." He easily lifted her, carrying her back to the bed and laying her down upon the edge. "And I intend to taste every inch of you."

Moisture pooled between her legs as his tongue slid roughly from her navel up to the hollow of her throat. His body covered hers, his tongue possessively invading her mouth. When Landen came up for air, she playfully nibbled his lower lip. Growling in response, he pinned her arms above her head.

Landen wasn't kidding about tasting all of her. His mouth moved to suck her fingers, slowly and sensuously. Allowed access to his chest, Chrissy decided to enjoy breakfast as well. She twirled her tongue around his nipple. Landen's hips bucked in response, but he didn't stop. Moving down some, he bit at her sensitive wrists before working down her arms.

Her body awakened beneath his, writhing, but he stilled her with a firm press of his legs. He nipped at the hollow of her throat before moving to lavish attention on her breast. The rough drag of his tongue across her nipple was maddening. He took the tight bud in his teeth and sucked harshly, leaving an aching void of sensation when he turned his attention to the other breast.

Kindly, he dropped a hand from Chrissy's wrists and began to explore further south, dipping a finger slowly in and out of her wet slit. A gasp earned her an additional finger as his tongue continued down her ribcage and his teeth found the sensitive spots on her hips.

Chrissy bit her lip in anticipation as he stilled over her mound. Landen wasn't ready to give in yet. Inhaling deeply, he released a hot, moist stream of air over her. When she twitched, he inhaled again and issued a moan of pleasure. The sound alone made Chrissy's sex clench. Wolf or not, this side of the detective was sexy and unexpected.

Her legs tried to close, in order to gain some friction and ease her torment, but were stopped by his body. She felt the pressure release on her wrists as he massaged her and placed kisses on the inside of her thighs.

She moaned as he removed his fingers from inside her, dropping to his knees at the side of the bed. His strong hands lifted her leg as his teeth grazed her instep and ankle. Chrissy's hips bucked and she looked through her eyelashes to find Landen smiling. He hooked her knees over his shoulders and plunged his tongue inside her.

"Fuck, Lan!" she screamed, unable to withstand the sheer pleasure he was inflicting on her body. He tongued her slit a few more times before lowering her knees and standing, offering a full view of his rigid cock. Landen's intense attention had been blissful agony for Chrissy. She had no idea how he'd been able to deny himself this long.

Predatorily, he crouched over her, crawling his way up her body. His slender fingers laced with hers as he entered her. Landen watched Chrissy's face intently for every reaction. His pace wasn't quick and needy like before, yet it was just as passionate.

Chrissy opened her mouth to gasp, but couldn't make a sound—so piercing was the sensation as Landen ground his hips in small circles. His forehead rested on hers and they both panted in need, their eyes gazing hungrily, tongues reaching out to tease lips.

Chrissy wanted to hold out for him, to let him come first, but in the end she couldn't. She shuddered as his thrusts grew more insistent. Over and over he pounded his hips against hers, forcing her to spiral through orgasm after orgasm. Finally, she felt a tremor run through his body as he lost himself, spilling his hot seed inside her.

She wasn't sure how long they lay there, silently locked together. Chrissy only knew that she didn't want to let go of Landen, or this feeling of contentment. However, the long summer day was well underway and they had errands to run before the evening.

After all, the wolf would not wait.

Chapter Six

Landen was stubbornly unwilling to move from the bed. When Chrissy tried to leave, he pulled her in close, burying his nose in her hair. With a little wrestling, a lot of giggling, and a few mock-scolds, she finally got him to release his hold.

To reward herself, Chrissy stood up and took a moment to appreciate the sight of him lying naked in her bed with an unabashedly satisfied grin on his baby face. "Much as I enjoyed your version of breakfast," she said, skirting away as he grabbed for her again, "we need to actually eat."

Landen rolled to the side of the bed and sat up with a groan, running a hand over his face and then through his mess of hair. Chrissy felt her stomach tighten and her heart speed up. Would she ever tire of watching him do that?

Pressing his palms onto his knees, Landen jumped up and enclosed her waist in his arms. "How about I whip something up for us then?" A gentle kiss fell on her forehead.

"All right, I'm going to grab some clothes from the car."

Landen's hands glided down to Chrissy's hips, pulling her back toward him. "But I like you naked and freshly fucked." He began swaying back and forth, pulling her into an impromptu dance that was all in his hips.

"Down boy," Chrissy teased, noting he was already at half- mast again. Landen's libido was even worse than hers. Apparently, once the detective was over his fear of the wolf, he was willing to reveal a playfully dominant side. She suppressed the urge to immediately push him back on the bed and explore this new revelation.

"I have half a mind to keep you handcuffed to my bed all day." He accentuated the statement with a sharp smack to her ass. The blow was hard enough to make her jump and issue a small yelp.

"Breakfast," she insisted with a laugh. Noticing his leer, she corrected herself. "Real breakfast first. I promise to keep you more than entertained later."

Landen released her with another swat. "I promise to hold you to that."

From the corner of her eye, Chrissy noticed him watching her as she bent over to grab her jeans from the floor and slide them on. When Landen bent her over again to grind his hips against her, she physically pushed him out the door toward the kitchen. She heard the rattle of pans as she searched for her shirt. Without locating her bra, she put the shirt on and walked out the front door barefoot.

Landen was sitting at the table when Chrissy came back in, his thumb idly toying with the rim of his coffee. He settled back in his chair, spreading those long legs wide, obviously enjoying the view as she walked over to drop her clothes on the end of the table. Chrissy hid a smile. He was so irresistible when he was happy.

His upbeat attitude, however, did not distract her from what he was eating.

Chrissy hopped on the table, bracing her bare feet on his chair exactly at that point where his low jeans were already tight again. She reached down to pluck the piece of bread from his hands. "Really, Landen? Just toast?"

Not moving his eyes from her chest, he pushed over a plate with a homemade egg and cheese bagel sandwich accompanied by a lovely mixture of fruit. Chrissy took a bite and closed her eyes, appreciatively savoring the experience. Damn, the man could cook.

She picked up a piece of pineapple and popped it in her mouth before noticing that he wasn't eating. "Where's yours?" she asked, covering her half-full mouth.

Landen raised his eyebrows and looked at her innocently. Pulling off a piece of the sandwich, she offered it to him. A roguish smile was on his face as he leaned forward to eat it from her fingers, his lips sucking greedily as they pulled away. Landen tried to inch closer, but the placement her foot prevented him from moving.

Two can play at this game, Chrissy thought wickedly. She traced the tuft of hair leading into his jeans before beginning to stroke him with the tips of her toes. Landen's head fell back in response.

"Are you going to make me feed you breakfast bit by bit?" she challenged, removing her foot.

His head raised and he eyed her for a moment before biting into her thigh. The unexpected savagery caused a tingle to surge through her. Landen's wicked grin told Chrissy that he smelled her arousal. Yes, the wolf was frisky this morning, but if she couldn't get Landen to eat he'd be irritable and uncontrollable later. It's was time to issue an ultimatum.

"Landen, I know you'd rather screw, but you need to eat." Chrissy hopped down from the table and ripped off another piece of the sandwich. She placed the bite between her teeth and pressed it to his mouth as she dipped down to straddle him on the chair. He took the morsel from her, reaching for her waist as he chewed. Chrissy swatted his hands away, leaning in close to the detective's ear. "If you don't finish what's on this plate in the next three minutes, you are going to miss out on some mind-blowing shower sex."

Instantly, she felt his interest peak beneath her. She stood, not giving him a chance to react. Without looking back, she sauntered toward the bedroom, peeling off her shirt along the way. "I'd hate to have to start without you."

Chrissy lazily walked into the bathroom and dropped her jeans to the floor. She had no doubt that the detective would follow her soon enough. Turning on the water, she let the room fill with steam before she stepped in and closed the glass door. Her muscles relaxed under the warmth, causing a soft involuntary moan to escape her lips before she realized she wasn't alone.

Dominant and voyeuristic, she noted mentally. Might as well give him a show then. Chrissy ran her hands over her stomach, pretending not to notice Landen staring though the glass. She stretched, lifting her arms and arching her back to feel the water cascade down her front. Bringing them back down, she turned, closing her eyes and massaging her shoulders in a way that concealed then revealed her breasts. Her fingers traveled down over her tits and between her legs, finding that nub of nerves and causing her to shiver.

Chrissy turned again as she leaned forward into the wall, hiding herself from his watchful gaze. She heard the door open then, and felt herself being pulled back hard against Landen's firm chest. Two long fingers delved deep inside her and she gasped.

"No," she murmured, grasping his wrist as his hands began to work their magic. He'd taken her twice already. She wanted to see him undone this time.

"No?" the word rumbled deep in Landen's throat. His fingers didn't stop searching, if anything his attentions increased. "You promised," he reminded, nudging her ear with his nose.

She cried out as he bit into her shoulder and scissored his fingers inside her. Rather than fight it, Chrissy reached back and stroked him firmly, starting a slow, deliberate rhythm that brought him to full erection almost immediately.

"I promised to give you mind-blowing shower sex," Chrissy reiterated, "but that's going to be difficult if I can't stand."

She felt a sudden emptiness as Landen removed his fingers. She began to turn but his hands seized hers, covering them and lifting her arms to cage her against the wall. His long limbs pulled her forward while his knee edged her feet wider apart. With one swift thrust, he buried himself inside her, stretching her with his girth. Chrissy's breath came in quick pants as Landen stayed motionless for what felt like an eternity. He then withdrew almost completely before thrusting in fully again.

"Can you feel me, love?"

Thrust, wait, withdraw. Thrust, wait, withdraw. The torturous sequence ensured that Chrissy felt nothing but him and the coil of desire burning within her.

"Yes," she hissed, whimpering as his next thrust hit her G-spot. Landen's hands never strayed from hers. His pace did not quicken. However, her need was steadily increasing. "Landen," she cried out, pleading.

"Chrissy, you are mine," he growled in her ear, the words punctuating his thrusts.

She understood that this was his wolf. Since she washed his scent from her body, he needed to mark her as his. She offered her neck in a show of submission. Strangely, he ignored the gesture.

"Mine," he stated again with another hard thrust. "Mine to mate. Mine to claim. Submit." Chrissy was used to having the upper hand with her lovers. Landen's sheer ferociousness had her at a loss. Even with other alphas, no one had ever asserted themselves so forcefully. It was primal.

Something stirred in her blood, responding to his aggression. She would give anything to please him, if she only knew what he needed. Amazing as Landen's cock felt, she wasn't sure how much longer her body could withstand the demanding nature of his lovemaking.

A cry ripped from Chrissy's lips, giving voice to the mix of pleasure and agony swimming through her as his relentless movements racked her body. Her legs grew weak as the teasing motions continued to promise release, but denied it.

"Say it, Chrissy," he urged, his voice softer, but expectant. "I need to hear you say it." "Yours," she choked out, tears spilling down her cheeks at the overload in sensation. "Oh

God, Lan. I am yours."

Landen's thrusts quickened and her body reacted at once, gyrating, searching for release. His hand snaked between her legs, his thumb and finger finding her clit and rolling it tenderly, pushing her past sanity. Chrissy's mind shattered as her body convulsed around him.

That was enough for Landen to find his own release. He pulled out swiftly, still hard as he turned Chrissy and pressed his mouth to hers. His arms offered support when she sagged, too overwhelmed to stand. His tongue licked gently at her lips as the water flowed over their bodies.

"You are mine, Chrissy," he repeated again, only tenderly this time, gazing deep into her eyes.

"Yours," she whispered.

She rested her head on his shoulder, enjoying the spray of the water as she tried to catch her breath. Even as she relaxed, Chrissy felt a tightening in her chest, an unfamiliar throb that was both slightly painful and utterly reassuring. For a second she wondered if this was what it felt like to be embraced by a mate, but she shoved the thought aside. If she and Landen were meant to be mates, Chrissy would've known months ago.

She'd thought she'd been mated before. When she was younger there had been a relationship with another Were that started intensely passionate. When it failed, Chrissy resigned to the fact that she would never find that kind of love again. Being a Skip made it too complicated. Still, this was how she had always imagined it would be, this type of connection. The force of what she felt with Landen was startling and just a bit unnerving.

Chrissy was brought back to the moment as Landen's fingers began to roam her body once more. The residual effects of their passion were wearing off and as her strength returned, she felt the sudden need to caress him. Chrissy lathered some shampoo and massaged it into Landen's scalp, enjoying the subtle intimacy of the act. If his smile was any indication, Landen was enjoying it as well.

The comfortable familiarity of the moment cut through her. There was so much he needed to learn, possibly in a very short time. Chrissy wondered if she would make it through all she had to tell him, all he needed to see. Would he still want her when he knew everything?

Chapter Seven

Chrissy's head was a bit muddled when they got out of the shower, but she brushed it off. Landen had gone back into the kitchen to tidy up, giving her a few precious moments to herself. She needed to focus. He had so much to learn, and she was hyper-aware that after this weekend he might not speak to her again.

Once he learns about my parents, once he knows what happened he won't want anything to do with me, she thought morosely, then hardened her resolve. If that was the case, today would be crucial.

Whatever was between them was secondary to making sure he learned to do more than simply survive his shifts. Landen had to start living with his wolf instead of fighting it. He had to enjoy being himself, all of himself, not just the human part. Chrissy needed to move forward methodically, without alerting Landen that she was hiding part of herself from him.

First, she had to teach him how to eat right. The man would not survive off toast and fish alone. From what she saw yesterday, he obviously loved to cook, so she'd start there. The trip to the butcher shop in Norway would give them the proper ingredients to make a few of her mom's best recipes, the ones that had been passed down for generations.

For a second, Chrissy remembered cooking with her mom and dad in the kitchen of the lake house. How often had they gathered in the heart of this house, laughing and chatting? If they were here, Mom would have been chopping veggies, arguing lightheartedly with Dad while he specially prepared rare venison steaks.

He would, of course, have insisted on teaching Landen how to prepare the meat to please both man and wolf. Chrissy could almost picture two of them chatting by the grill, the summer sun illuminating their smiling faces while they discussed the best cut and cooking temperature.

Dad had always been slow warming to anyone new in Chrissy's life, but she was certain Mom would have instantly loved Landen. What would it have been like for Landen to learn with her family?

Quickly, Chrissy pushed the reverie away.

She couldn't keep thinking about her family any more than she could continue dwelling on a relationship that had no future. She needed the separation. Her heart had almost recovered from the loss of her pack. Chrissy wasn't sure it would heal again if she allowed things to progress too far with Landen. A risk, a fling, was fine. But thinking about him with family — considering him a mate — was more than a risk, it was suicide.

Knowing the market closed early on Saturday, Chrissy plaited her damp hair and hustled to find clothes. Unfortunately, she hadn't found an extra shirt in the car earlier so she riffled though the drawers and came up with one of Landen's. The striped button-down smelled like him. Inhaling deeply, she slid it over her head.

As the garment covered her face, her mind rattled off all the other items to go through while she still had time: Control, enough to avoid hurting anyone, anyway. Basic signs to recognize other wolves. They'd gone through some brief terminology last night.

"Ooh. I like that, love."

Her thoughts were interrupted as she pulled her braid from the collar. Turning, she found Landen had returned from the kitchen. He was leaning against the door, dressed in his usual low-slung jeans, a checked button-down, and a denim jacket. His tone said neither of them would stay dressed if she didn't get him out of the house.

"It's just temporary," she warned with a mock-glare. "I'll stop by the cabin after our errands to get some of my own clothes. Now, move!" She shooed him. "We have to get to the butcher's before one."

Surprisingly, he didn't argue.

The half-hour ride into town was blissful. The sun streamed through the open window and Chrissy relaxed as she drove, the warm breeze whipping around her. They hardly talked, but Landen seemed much more at ease. His hand

gripped hers lightly and rested on her leg. Both of their spirits were high after that morning.

When they pulled up to the market, Landen squeezed her hand and placed a brief kiss on her temple. Chrissy's heart pounded in her chest. The gesture was sweet and easy; he seemed at home with her. This Landen was so different from the usual Detective Sutherlund who kept a tight rein on his emotions. She wondered if this is what he was like before the accident. Was it being turned that put the intense melancholy behind his eyes?

Landen said something about meeting her in the store in a few minutes, but Chrissy was too preoccupied to catch where he was going instead. It was already noon. Worried about the time frame, she let him go without clarification.

"*Älskling* ," she was greeted when she walked into the small, but busy store. The little bell on the shop door clinked as she pushed it shut behind her.

"Mama Engel." Chrissy stepped behind the counter to give the thin, grey-haired woman a hug. "You look more beautiful every time I see you."

"Pure flattery, sweeting," Chrissy's friend replied before returning her attention to the line of customers in front of her. The shop was thick with summer tourists getting items they'd forgotten for their camping trips. "But you know I enjoy it. You are late today. Would that be because of the handsome man with you in the car?"

Chrissy blushed. "Oh, Landen? I—" She wasn't sure what to say. She liked him, but other than shape-shifting and mind-blowing sex, they hadn't talked much about their relationship. After this weekend, anyways, there likely wouldn't be a relationship at all.

"It's okay. I won't pry."

That was part of the reason Mama Engel had been so close to Chrissy's family. Mama Engel had an intimate, though platonic, relationship with Grandpa Torsten. Very few of Grandma's friends had stuck around after she'd passed, but Mama Engel had helped Grandpa raise Chrissy's mom. The strong Swedish woman had been the first to call Chrissy after she'd returned home. Though not wolves themselves, Mama and Joseph knew her family's secrets just as she knew theirs. They would never be her pack, but they were the closest thing Chrissy had left of family in this part of the country.

"With extra company, I'm guessing you'll need a bit more than the usual?"

"Double, actually," Chrissy added sheepishly, hating to complicate things last minute when the store was already busy. If only Landen had been less insistent this morning they would have been in sooner. Not that she'd minded at the time.

"Joseph!" Mama Engel cried over the buzz in the store. "Double the order for *min favorit.*"

"Yes, *Mormor.*" Mama Engel's adorably buff grandson peaked above the butcher counter, his spiky blond-tipped hair and perfectly scruffy face attracting the attention of every female in the shop. He smiled and waved, earning Chrissy the stink-eye from at least three girls waiting in line.

"Give me about fifteen, okay, Chrissy?"

Both to get away from the girls and to pass some time, Chrissy decided she might as well pick up a few other things while she was here. Grabbing a basket she headed to the produce section. She was picking up some peppers when a familiar voice sounded behind her.

"This surely can't be a coincidence, running into you here." Landen was all smiles, standing with a basket in his hand. She smiled back, glad to see he was still in good humor.

"Don't play shy," he continued, maneuvering himself closer to her. "Turning up where I always get away," his hand reached to finger the collar of her shirt, "and wearing my clothes, no less. You know, I've noticed it's always you who brings up files when I call."

Chrissy's stomach did a flip. It was fun and surprising to see this many facets of Landen in such a short time. From worried and needy, to obsessive and possessive, and now playful. Who knew he was into roleplaying? Chrissy hoped she wouldn't have to see him go back to brooding.

"Oh Detective, I had no idea you were in town this weekend," she responded, her voice dropping to a whisper. "Are you stalking me?"

His eyes glittered when he saw she was willing to play along and Landen pressed forward with the game. "Stalking? I don't think I'd call it that. Though I can't say I'm sorry I ran into you." He by inching a bit closer, leaning his chest forward to brush her back while pretending to inspect the vegetables. "What do you think about coming to my place? Let me earn back my shirt by doing unspeakable things to your delectable body."

"Enticing," she replied. Her body responded, too. She was already quivering at the thought of him inside again. Still, this was a game and she didn't want to make it too easy. "Too bad for you I just met someone last night, and I'm not sure you could compete. He's pretty amazing in bed."

"Really?" Landen's jeans were getting noticeably tighter in the front, and Chrissy could smell the earthy fragrance of his arousal coming off him in waves. It made her knees go weak and a tingle shoot straight to her core.

She'd never had this type of reaction to anyone before. Why was it so impossible to get enough of him? It was thrilling and, at the same time, a bit disconcerting. She chalked it up to the spike in her libido that always came with the full moon, and the fact that she'd been watching the detective for so long.

Getting her head back in the game, she tried to play off her need.

"You'd better watch out. He's kind of a beast when he gets jealous." For a second worry flashed in Landen's bright eyes, but it disappeared quickly enough that Chrissy thought she must have imagined it.

"Then why isn't he here?" Landen's hand slipped into the back pocket of her jeans, and he squeezed her ass. "Anyone could just put their hands all over you."

"Chrissy!" Joseph called from the counter, interrupting their fun. "Hey babe, whenever you're ready."

Again, she got a couple of nasty looks from the tourists, but not nearly as blatantly ugly as the one Landen gave Joseph. Chrissy's stomach fell as she watched Landen's posture shift from easy to aggressive. Being the afternoon of the full moon, Chrissy worried about the kind of trouble an agitated wolf might cause in the middle of a busy grocery store. But for a moment she also let herself consider that his reaction might be more than the protective nature of a Were. With all we've experienced together in the last twenty-four hours, is it possible Landen is jealous, she wondered. She opened her mouth to reassure the handsome detective and diffuse the situation, but Landen quieted her, possessively pressing a hand to her back and ushering her to the meat counter.

"Why don't you introduce us, *babe?*" The word sounded wrong coming out of Landen's mouth. Out of the corner of her eye, Chrissy watched his jaw stiffen.

Joseph must not have noticed the tension because he came around the glass counter with the bags, and handed them over before pulling her into a one-armed hug. "You should stop by to see us more often," Joseph chided, squeezing her tight around the shoulders. "*Mormor* misses you."

Landen cleared his throat and took the bags from Chrissy.

"Joseph," the butcher introduced himself, releasing her and extending his hand to the taller man.

Chrissy watched her blithe Landen slip back to surly Detective Sutherlund as he grasped Joseph's hand with what had to be a bone-crushing pressure. "Landen," he growled, darkly. Chrissy winced, but Joseph laughed musically, pulling away.

"Nice grip. I'd tell you to be good to my babygirl here, but I've seen her drop anyone not worth her time. If she's planning on making you dinner, I gotta figure you're okay."

"Thank you for the approval," Landen's tone carried no warmth. "Actually, I plan on cooking her dinner this evening. A lady should be treated to a nice meal." His arm draped over Chrissy's shoulders, but it felt more like a sign of ownership than affection.

It took significant effort for her not to push him away, but she waited, giving Landen the opportunity to redeem himself before she created a scene in front of her friend.

"Agreed." Joseph responded with a huge smile. "But I don't count Chrissy here as a lady. She beat the snot out of me too many times as a kid. Babygirl, if my girlfriend only knew how you tried to ruin this beautiful face."

At that, the frosty Detective Sutherlund melted back into Landen's relaxed stance. His hand caressed her shoulder lightly then dropped to catch hers. She looked over to see him glancing guiltily at the bag in his hand.

Relieved, Chrissy sighed and nudged Joseph with her elbow. "You always deserved it." "Probably. Never learned to steer clear of women who could kick my butt. Speaking of

which…" He nodded to the register. Looking over, Chrissy smiled when she saw Mama Engel was shooting Joseph a look that clearly said he'd better get back to work. "Good luck with this one, Landen."

Now that he'd cooled down, Chrissy noticed Landen was on his best behavior. He brought the bags to the counter and made sure to compliment Mama Engel on her wonderful store. Chrissy could tell Mama was pleased with the detective.

She gave Chrissy a little wave when they walked away, and winked when Landen laced his fingers through Chrissy's on the way out the door.

Once outside, Chrissy placed the groceries into the cooler in the trunk of her car. "You know, when I said the guy I met last night was a bit jealous, I was joking. Joseph's like my little brother. You could have checked with me before trying to break his hand."

"Sorry," Landen mumbled. "Not a trait I'm proud of."

She crossed her arms across her chest and stared levelly at him. "Your temper, have you only had it since you were turned?"

He shook his head.

"All right. Is it worse now?"

"I didn't want to find out. It's why I've been," he paused, and she knew he was thinking about the tranquilizers she'd destroyed. "It's why I've locked myself away every month. It was bad enough before."

Chrissy knew there was something he wasn't telling her, but decided now wasn't the time to pursue it. The only guy she'd ever seen get riled up like that was her father. He'd been a bit overbearing when offended, and Mom had called him out on it more than a few times. Those conversations had always worked better when approached with understanding.

Taking that into consideration, she rose up on her toes and gave Landen a peck on the cheek, surprising him. "We'll figure it out. Running will help," she promised. Her eyes took on a devilish look. "But we have more important things to discuss now."

"Really?"

She could tell his interest was piqued. "Yep. It's time to go home, and you have yet to convince me that you deserve this shirt back." She turned to walk to the driver's side door and yelped as Landen's fingers grabbed the loops of her jeans to pull her back.

"Keys," he demanded.

She handed them over, wondering what he had in mind, but let him take the wheel. They were barely out of town when he grabbed her hand and pulled it by his thigh, rubbing small circles into the back of it with his thumb.

"So, tell me more about this new lover and his skills," Landen prompted. Chrissy raised an eyebrow. "I have to know if I'm going to earn my shirt back. Be *very* detailed."

Well, she figured, he asked for it. Chrissy had no intention of going easy on him, especially not after that little stunt in the store. "He's such an animal," she began. "With every touch he has complete possession of my body. His hands fit perfectly over my breasts, and feel rough and firm when he cups them around my ass to pull me into his thrusts. And his cock, mmm."

Her voice got huskier as she thought of Landen listening to her talk about his skills. Her body began reacting, desire pooling between her legs. She continued along the same lines, praising his ferocity, his physical prowess, and his tender affection.

Landen's hand released hers and reached over to unbutton her jeans. Gently, he took Chrissy's fingers off his thigh and slid them down into her panties. He waited until both their fingers brushed over her sensitive button, making her moan before removing his hand and replacing it on the wheel. Slowly, she began circling her finger, rubbing her clit until he moved them again, nudging her fingers inside her.

On its way back to the steering wheel, Chrissy noticed Landen's hand brushed the rather prominent bulge in his jeans. Knowing this was getting to him was a huge turn on, she decided to change tactics.

"The first time he took me was utterly intense," she moaned. "He was wild, ravaging my body with his tongue before he took his perfect cock and rammed into me so deep that I can almost still feel him inside me. God, it was so sweet. He knew just where to touch me and when we came together...*ohhhhhh*." She shuddered, just thinking about it.

By the time they reached the house, Chrissy's clothing was soaked and Landen practically threw himself out of the car. He was beside her door in an instant, his body pinning Chrissy to the metal. His mouth invaded hers. Their tongues twined together, and she couldn't resist snaking her leg up around his perfect hips.

With a jerk he pulled away, leaving her breathless and off balance. "You are entirely too good at this," Landen growled. He lifted her easily, slinging her over his shoulder.

"Landen!" she cried, seeing the house recede behind them and not knowing where he was taking her.

He responded with a firm swat to her ass, making her squeak. His long strides easily carried them to spot where he shifted the first evening. Gingerly, Landen set Chrissy down and pulled off his jacket before sinking to the grass, and guiding her to rest on top of him.

For a few moments, he searched her eyes. Those nimble fingers caressed the side of her face before reaching to her long, brown braid and unwinding it. Landen's hands ran through her still damp hair, releasing it to the winds that played along the top of the cliff that dropped to the lake.

Rolling up his jacket, he lay back on the ground, placing it beneath his head. Still he stared at her. Finally, he grabbed her hand, brushing his fingers across her skin. She shivered at the slight tickle.

"God, how can you be so perfect, Chrissy?"

The question took her by surprise.

"Landen," She sighed, rolling her eyes. "I'm not..."

"Yes, you are," he insisted. "I knew it the first time Cavanaugh brought you into the department. Your hair was doing that cute thing where it half falls out of your ponytail and you brush it behind your ear. It was the middle of January and you smelled like summer." He paused, bringing her hand to his lips and kissing it. "You still do."

"Such a smooth talker when you want to get laid," she said, smiling and tweaking his nose with her finger. "If I recall correctly, the first time you met me, Cavanaugh had to tell you to quit being such an asshole. I'd hate to have seen your attitude if I'd been a little less perfect."

"Self-defense." Landen responded sheepishly.

"Right," she agreed sarcastically. "Because I am obviously the hostile one. It took me over a month to get you to even look at me and four more to make you open up."

"And when I finally let you in," Landen grinned, kneading his thumbs into her hips, "you had me on my knees in half an hour. Chrissy," he sighed, "What did I do to deserve you?"

She brushed a hand over his chest, letting it rest over his heart. "How can you see so much beauty in me and none of it in yourself?" When he tried to turn his head away, she caught his chin and made him look at her. "Landen, you are strong and compassionate. I've heard you talk a mother down after she learned her child died in a hit-and-run. I watched you almost tranq yourself to keep from hurting anyone. People don't do that without caring about others." She stopped herself before admitting out loud that these were ideal qualities in a mate.

Landen placed his hand over hers. "You see the best in me. But I didn't become a detective because I cared about people. I was in it to prove I was better, smarter. God, I'm glad you didn't know me before. My temper, my arrogance. You'd have looked right past me."

Chrissy knew she couldn't have. She'd have been just as attracted to Landen.

"By the time you showed up, I'd shut out everyone. Bridge had been ragging on me for months and all you had to do was walk through the door. Consequences be damned, I wanted to grab you right there in the office, but I'd been dealing with the wolf for over a year and there was no way I was going to let you get close to me. I'd already..." he choked up. "I wasn't going to hurt you."

Her heart clenched. He'd resisted the pull for so long. He was stronger than he knew, and when he learned her secret he would leave. She had to stop this. But, damn everything, she didn't want to. Leaning down, Chrissy rested her forehead on his. "There's so much you don't know."

"I don't care," he insisted. "I'll never be good enough to be worthy of you." She started to interject, but Landen stilled her lips with a kiss. "We can talk about that later. Right now, let me make love to you. Please, Chrissy. Before tonight, before the wolf takes over, just let me love you."

She needed no further urging to slide her jeans down. Landen pulled himself free, giving her full access to him. She was so wet from the car ride it took nothing for her to guide him inside. His hands carefully undid the buttons of her shirt, exposing her breasts to the sunlight and his touch.

The need was there, as always; Chrissy could feel his body calling to hers. This time she took charge, undulating her hips. The feel of the sunlight on her skin and Landen between her thighs was intoxicating. It was simple, raw, and exquisite.

"Lan," she breathed, ignoring her conflicting emotions and dropping her head back to revel in the bliss of the moment.

"Yes, love." He shifted, sitting up to hold her closer. The change let her take him even deeper. Landen's teeth ghosted across her neck and collarbone making her shudder.

At that moment something inside her snapped. She felt it jolt through her body, an electrifying sensation that pulled her even closer to him.

Chrissy grabbed for Landen's hand, feeling comforted when his rose to meet hers. Their fingers locked as their lips met, releasing them both from anything but joining together in the moment. It took so little for him to push her over the edge, and when she went, he followed, their bodies collapsing upon each other.

Breathing heavily, Chrissy pulled her hand away to run it through Landen's growing curls and looked into his eyes. Those bottomless pools were filled with honeyed flecks and concern.

Oh God, she was in trouble.

Chapter Eight

His eyes were fully golden when they returned to the house. Chrissy marveled at how controlled Landen was for being so far into his transformation. With no training prior to yesterday and only the tranquilizers to keep his instincts previously at bay, his persistence of will was nothing short of amazing. Apparently they didn't need to discuss control. Few others would have been able to handle Landen's situation without breaking in two.

A feeling of pride swelled inside Chrissy's chest. Her mate was strong. The feeling swiftly turned to worry. Where had that thought come from? She could not be mated to Landen. When he found out her secret, he would leave. She wouldn't be able to handle it.

As if sensing her thoughts, Landen pressed his hand to the small of her back. Even with no one else around he was protective and commanding. There was a stern and concentrated slant to his eyes, causing that wrinkle in his forehead. In response, Chrissy slipped her hand in his back pocket and squeezed.

Landen grabbed the groceries from the trunk and took them inside, letting Chrissy teach him how to make the perfect venison burgers. Late lunch was an easy affair. He enjoyed the venison like she knew he would and it would keep up his strength far better than whatever he'd been subsiding on each month, which made her happy.

Chrissy made a mental note to keep a closer eye on his diet now that he was part of her pack. Even if everything ended this weekend, she owed him that. She'd make sure that the Engels had an order for Landen each month, and she'd root through his bag to make sure she'd disposed of all those damn tranquilizers in case he got any stupid ideas again.

They were finishing up the dishes together when Chrissy realized that she still hadn't made it to the cabin for clothes. She would need to grab those tonight as she was in second-day jeans and Landen's shirt.

She casually bumped his hip as he pulled a plate from the soapy water. "I need to run to the cabin when we're done, to grab a few things. It shouldn't take long," she let him know as she rinsed the dish and placed it on the rack.

"Sure, love." Landen dried his arms and rolled his sleeves down before wiping his hands on his jeans. "Is it close, or are we taking the car?"

"We?" Chrissy raised an eyebrow and crossed her arms.

"Of course. You're not going into those woods alone. I'm not letting you out of my sight."

Chrissy understood he was trying to be protective. Her dad used to be the same way. Still, it made her cringe. These were her woods and had been since she was a little girl. She knew the placement of every rock in the lake's cliff side, and could ferret out the den of every animal hiding in the underbrush of the forest. She'd been perfectly fine protecting herself up to now and being considered a frail female was irritating.

"Landen," she sighed. "I am perfectly capable..."

"Of attracting any other Were near these woods. I assume we're not the only ones." His nose brushed the length of her arm as he inhaled deeply. "You have such a delectable scent." His eyes flashed. "And it's stronger now that I've fucked you. You are mine. I'll be damned if I'm letting anyone else near you."

That bristle she'd been feeling seconds before melted into a whole different type of sensation. How many times could she sleep with this man before he stopped being able to turn her into a puddle with a few words and a look? It was all she could do to nod in response.

Twenty minutes later, they had walked to the cabin. It was a small, cozy thing, not much more than one central room with exposed beams, a central wood-burning stove, and a small bathroom. But it had been perfect for Chrissy's monthly getaways.

Heading directly toward the wardrobe, Chrissy pulled out a backpack and some clothes. She'd assumed Landen would stay outside, but she soon heard him enter through the front door. His boots made determined thumps along the wooden floor, letting Chrissy know exactly where each long stride has taken him. He'd stopped by the bed. She tried to ignore that bit of knowledge.

"I love watching you," he said casually, creating a bit of a squeak when he settled down on the mattress. "Everything about you is beautiful. Those strong shoulders. Those curvy hips. That round ass. Your movements are sleek, powerful, seductive, and you seem completely unaware of it. It's breathtaking."

Chrissy glanced over her shoulder to see him leaned back on his elbows with his legs stretched out. Indeed, a look of sincere appreciation was on Landen's face and that pink tongue darted sinfully over his bottom lip. Chrissy decided it was time to set things straight.

"Detective Sutherlund, you say the most inappropriate things to me."

Landen cocked an eyebrow, smiling as she strode toward him. Chrissy could smell his wolfish essence growing stronger. With only a short time until moonrise, both of them were feeling the effects. Landen was almost feral—everything but shifted. Chrissy wondered how long this scent would linger, and then pushed the thought away, unwilling to consider him leaving.

"You think I'm unaware of my effect on you?"

In seconds she had straddled his hips, pressing his face to her chest as she breathed him in. His eyes were a bit glazed when she released him. Her arms draped casually around his neck as she pressed her forehead to his.

"You can't hide it. You smell deliciously masculine when you are horny. Every good bitch knows how to elicit that response from an alpha male." Chrissy's tongue darted out to lick his lips, but she withdrew when he opened his mouth for a kiss. "Take off your shirt," she commanded, rising off his body. "Let me show you how an Alpha is treated in my pack."

Landen complied and Chrissy bit her lip, enjoying the feeling of his bare chest under her hands. Dropping to the floor, she roughly pulled off his boots then yanked down his jeans and boxers in one swift jerk. Now was not the time to be gentle.

Before he could move, she pushed those long legs apart and dipped between them, running her tongue along his length. Landen's head rolled back and an appreciative moan escaped. Chrissy swirled her tongue over the thick tip before fisting him at the base of his shaft and taking the rest in her mouth. This late on a full moon she knew it wouldn't take much to rile him up and Landen did not disappoint. Her mouth had only bobbed up and down a few times when his fingers twined in her hair, pulling her away.

"Stop," he growled. "You don't want—"

"Not like this. Take. Off. Your. Clothes. "

Chrissy stood, licking her lips pointedly and keeping herself positioned between his spread legs. She peeled off her jeans, placing a kiss on his cock when she bent to drop them to the floor. Landen rose to a sitting position, slipping one hand up her shirt to massage her breasts roughly and snaking the other down to check her already drenched folds. His need was taking over.

When he stood, his hands flowed back to Chrissy's waist, lifting her. Instinctively, she wrapped her legs around him. Her lips were on his neck, his chest, any part of him her tongue could reach. Landen was panting when his body slammed hers against the wall. The head of his cock teased at Chrissy's entrance, but he waited. Even this far gone in his desire, he waited.

"Please, Lan," she begged in his ear. "Take what's yours."

She couldn't hold back a scream as he plunged deep inside. Her body stretched, aching to take more of him. She found her hands reaching to the exposed beam above, grasping for purchase as he began a punishing rhythm. Landen tore at her shirt, ripping off the buttons and exposing her breasts to his tongue. The air made them stiffen, and he lapped and sucked at her nipples with such fierce tenderness that tears dripped down Chrissy's face.

She had never known a lover so attuned to her needs. He ravished her whole body with his, fingers slipping into the small of her spine, teeth nipping at her collarbone, hips driving her into the cabin wall. No piece of her escaped his attention. There was no sensation in her but what he provided and his hunger to have her was insatiable.

She dropped her arms from the beam as a whimper escaped her lips. She needed to caress this wounded animal, hold him closer as he drove inside her. It was a feeling so overwhelming that she almost couldn't breathe for the pressure in her chest. Chrissy's fingers raked through Landen's hair as she leaned in for a searing kiss.

Once his mouth met hers, she grabbed his shoulders, pulling him toward her with all her strength. Without knowing how, Chrissy recognized that this was what it was to be possessed by your mate. This was the unbridled pleasure each moon offered when the wolf awoke. It was how she would always know he was hers.

"Come for me, Chrissy," he demanded in a husky voice. She couldn't have resisted him if she'd wanted to. Her body approached the precipice, her muscles tensing around him as he drove her past the point of no return. The waves of pleasure rolled over her, causing her to shudder as he continued to push.

"Yours," Chrissy whispered. "Lan, my mate, my love, I am yours."

Those words shot the detective toward his release. Landen cried out as she took him in, all emotion wrapped in his upcoming shift and his need possess her. His body sagged against Chrissy's, his pants hot in her ear. She felt him move, carrying her to the couch before sitting and letting her body fall on top of his.

She straddled him, fluttering kisses across his face, his eyes, sweetly and languidly thanking him for his love. Her heart was full to bursting and her body radiated the joy of their joining. Landen moved slightly, shifting her weight to cradle her in his lap. Chrissy's arms looped around his neck as he let his head fall across her chest. She knew they could both lie like this forever, but all too soon it ended.

"I need—" Landen began.

Chrissy looked into to his almost glowing golden eyes. "I know," she murmured, and she did. The sun had already dropped below the trees. She knew he was worried about shifting in the cabin. Rapidly, she changed, picking up his clothes and stuffing them with a few other essentials into the backpack she had left near the wardrobe.

"Time to run," she told him and within minutes they were.

The moon was almost out of the sky when Chrissy pulled up to the lake, her breath coming in short pants and her legs burning with the effort of her exertion. Stretching, she dropped down to the grass and pulled off her shoes to let the water splash over her feet. Looking out, she reflected on how serene the lake was at night when the steam rose from the warm water to drape everything in an ethereal haze.

Shrugging off her backpack, Chrissy reached inside for a bottle of water and downed it in a few quick gulps. She was putting the empty bottle back into her pack when a noise caught her attention. She turned just in time to be knocked flat on her back by a massive tawny wolf. His front paws rested on her chest as warm, amber eyes gazed into hers.

"Yes, you got me, you damn showoff." Chrissy reached to run her hand through his pelt, unable to restrain her laughter when the wolf's tongue lolled out of his mouth. "Now, are you going to get off me? You're not exactly a lightweight."

Indeed, Landen was concentrated lean muscle and he responded to her comment by dropping his solid lupine body completely across hers. The good news was he was retaining human thought and reaction during the height of his
transformation. The bad news was that knowing this didn't make it any easier for Chrissy to move. She rolled her eyes and Landen huffed a few times. Chrissy immediately recognized that she was being laughed at.

"Seriously you obnoxious ton of fluff, get off me," she half-yelled, half-giggled at him. Even as the words left her lips, the moon dipped below the horizon and Landen shifted to

human. His naked form pressed to her half-clothed body, his legs tangled around hers. He was still laughing as he pushed himself up to hover above her. "Really, Chrissy? You didn't seem to mind this much earlier."

She found it hard to reply. It was thrilling to see the usually serious detective actually laughing, and yet another feeling was welling up within her. A connection she had never felt before had cemented itself within her at the cabin, and much as the run had helped clear her mind, it had not cleared her emotions.

Landen took advantage of her speechlessness by dipping down to probe her mouth open with his tongue. His scent enveloped her sweaty body, and his mouth tasted like ripe summer berries. It was the taste that brought her out of the moment.

She really needed to be more careful about keeping track of him. His sexual appetite had distracted her from his nutrition, and they'd been well into the run before her stomach rumbled, reminding her that dinner had been left uncooked back at the house.

Luckily, she remembered a patch of edible wild berries in the woods, and it'd been easy enough to convince Landen to stop running long enough to eat. She did not want to be responsible for his human stomach reacting to raw wild game if the wolf got too hungry. The day-after effects of a wolf's meal were not particularly pleasant.

"Landen Sutherlund, what am I going to do with you?" she asked when he finally let her breathe. Chrissy pushed a rogue curl back from his forehead. Even in the glimmer of pre-dawn she could see his eyes already flecking with their usual brilliant blue.

"Hopefully something dirty," he murmured, nuzzling at her neck.

Playfully brushing her arms along his back, she realized they were both covered in dust and cobwebs from running through the woods all night. Chrissy's attention shifted to the mist-covered lake.

"Mmmmm," she rumbled. "Maybe something clean this time."

With a slight push up on his chest, she convinced the detective to roll off of her. As she stood and striped off her clothes, she watched him lean back on his arms and run his tongue along his lips — a habit she loved. In the span of a few seconds, her bra and jeans sat in a neat little pile on the shore. She could feel his eyes watching her as she dipped into the lake.

The warm water swelled around her, easing her sore muscles from the long run. The lake was an enchanted place in the early hours. Taking a deep breath, Chrissy ducked under the surface, relishing in the weightless feeling and pushing her body until her lungs felt as if they might burst.

A few strong kicks and she glided silently to the surface. She instantly indulged the desire to dip back under. Her mother always said Chrissy'd be part otter if she wasn't all wolf. The thought brought a sharp pain in her chest. She wished her mother was here to talk her through this current predicament.

The splashing by the shore let Chrissy know Landen was worried. Between the dark, the mist, and her lung capacity, he must have lost sight of her. The sloshing of his long legs in the water gave her his exact location, and she decided it was time to enact some revenge for his actions on the shore. A few silent kicks brought her directly behind the detective, and before he knew she was there, Chrissy had wrapped her arms around his muscled torso, pulling him backward into the lake.

When he finally disengaged himself from her grasp Landen bobbed to the surface, drenched and sputtering. "Fuck me!" Wolfishly, he shook his head, flinging droplets from his doused curls, and running a hand over his face.

"All right."

Chrissy took only a second to savor his look of confusion before ducking under the water to brush around then swim through his long legs. Barely giving him time to recover, she dipped again and took another pass, this time skimming her fingers over his torso as she went by. When she glided up behind him, Landen was excited, tensed, and waiting to see where she planned on taking this. She loved keeping him on edge.

With one arm, Chrissy reached around his chest and up to his shoulder, pulling him slightly closer to shore and flush against her naked chest. Her other hand swam down to stroke his cock, causing his body to jerk in surprise, then go slack in her arms. They were both weightless, floating as his head dipped back and pressed into her shoulder. She ran her hand up and down his length in the warm water. With a groan Landen pulled away, twisting to face her.

The sun was skimming through the trees, offering enough light for Chrissy to see the naked hunger in his eyes, still when he reached for her his embrace was gentle. Landen pulled her head to his chest, letting the two of them drift in their own world in the water, feeling one another breathe. After what seemed like an eternity, he lifted her chin and placed on her lips a, sensual kiss that washed away every other sensation. Chrissy's head was spinning when he finally released her.

"Much as I'd love to take you here, we're both tired and the house is still a bit of a walk. Let's dry off and head back. I want to fall asleep with you in my arms, and ravish you when I wake."

If anything could pull her from the delicious embrace of the warm lake, that invitation would be it. Gliding to shore, Chrissy pulled a few towels out of her bag, tossing one to Landen as he rose from the water. Within minutes they were dry, dressed, and heading up the hill to the house hand-in-hand.

As they neared the house, she realized that sunrise meant this was the third day. Tonight would be the last night he shifted. A sick feeling swept over her when she thought about sharing her secret. Yet she had to tell him. What would it mean? The last two nights had been perfect.

Would he go back to being the brooding, evasive detective? After the last few days, Chrissy knew she'd never be able to handle that.

Landen seemed lost in his own thoughts as well. A line creased his forehead. When he looked over and caught her staring, his expression changed. Sensing her unease, Landen cocked an eyebrow at her as they walked in the door.

"All right, love?"

Chrissy nodded and mumbled something about being tired. His strong arms lifted her, carrying her to the bedroom. It did nothing to ease the ache in her chest.

"Lan," she whimpered as he set her down on the bed and removed her clothing. She felt a kiss on her temple and the covers tucked around her. A quiet rustling let her know that Landen was removing his own clothes. Soon after, she felt his warm body pressed against hers.

"Chrissy?" he murmured. Concern was clear in his voice, but so was fatigue. Chrissy counted on the latter giving her time.

She promised herself she wouldn't let him see her cry. Whatever happened when they woke, she didn't want him to pity her nor feel any guilt. It was a difficult promise to keep as a few tears escaped. Chrissy used her last bit of effort to keep her voice from shaking.

"Just... hold me. Please."

His strong arms pulled her into his chest and she took a deep breath, trying to burn the memory of him into her mind. To forget the strength of his embrace, his musky smell tinged with lake water, even the slight concerned hitch in his breathing, would kill her. She could lose him if she could just keep the moment.

Her brain betrayed her, mulling over everything she wanted to ignore. She knew that Landen was a wolf the second she'd walked into Homicide. How could she have guessed her connection to his transformation, or what would happen between them? After tonight she knew he was her alpha, her one true mate.

After a several long minutes, Chrissy's exhausted body overtook her mind. When they woke, she would deal with her feelings and all the confusion. She would enjoy her last day in his arms, knowing that at least now he would be safe to shift.

Chrissy would die inside when she told him the truth, and released him from any unnecessary feelings of obligation. She would handle everything then. For now, she simply slept, wrapped tightly around the one she loved.

Chapter Nine

The box was unusually heavy in Chrissy's arms as she trudged up the steps to Homicide. Landen had left the house that morning after the lake before giving her a chance to explain. She'd woken up to an empty bed, with no indication he'd been there other than his lingering scent on the sheets.

Chrissy hadn't seen him in nearly a week now. She'd found excuses to ignore that particular department, but today they were short-staffed and nobody else had time to take the files up. She'd been neglecting it since early that morning, but Cavanaugh had mentioned three times that Homicide was waiting.

Thursday morning department meetings usually lasted until eleven, so she'd hoped everyone would still be in the conference room. No such luck. Bridgette was sitting on Sutherlund's desk, chatting amicably with her partner when Chrissy opened the door. The smile dropped off Landen's face when he saw her.

"Oswin murder and background on Holocker," was all Chrissy could say.

Sensing the tension, Detective Bergin kindly mentioned something about coffee and slipped away with apologetic glance toward Chrissy. Landen's eyes flicked up and away. She noticed they were back to solid blue. They wouldn't be amber flecked again for a month.

"Are we going to talk?" she sighed, setting the boxes down. When she didn't get an answer, she tried again. "Over drinks, if here's not good?"

"Look, last weekend was great and I appreciate what you did, but quite honestly it's not going to work. That whole thing. I just..."

His hand ran though those glorious blond curls, making her remember what it was like when her fingers were woven in them, and his hands were all over her body. Tears began forming in her eyes, but she refused to let him see. A week ago, she promised him he wouldn't hurt her. But then she didn't think it was possible. Now, he was gradually killing her. Wolves mate for life and her mate had no interest in their connection.

"Chrissy, I appreciate all you did. You're the only one who understands what this is like. Once a month I become a monster. Apparently, the monster likes you."

"And what about you, Detective?" she whispered, already knowing the answer. "I just don't."

The words stabbed her in the heart.

With a gasp Chrissy's eyes flew open. The clock said 10 a.m. and Landen was still curled around her body, enveloping her in his heat. She knew four hours of sleep wouldn't get her through today, but she also knew she wouldn't get any rest after that dream. Slowly, carefully, Chrissy extracted herself from Landen's arms and pulled a pair of panties from the backpack and one of Landen's shirts from the floor. Quietly, she padded into the kitchen to put on the kettle. She needed some tea.

Today. She had to tell him today. Her mind ran through the scenarios, all of them bad, and her stomach churned. She caught the kettle before it whistled. The last thing she needed was the shrill noise to alert Landen that she'd gone. After grabbing a mug, Chrissy headed out the door to sit on the porch.

The lake had a different effect in the morning. No longer was it a misty mermaid lagoon. In the morning light, with the sun glittering gold on the water's ripples, it was a reflection of the floor of heaven. Unfortunately, neither image would help push Landen from her thoughts.

She could still feel his gentle hands exploring her body and his breath ghosting at her ear. Her mouth still tasted him and, oh God, his smile. Her breath escaped in a choked noise as she curled up in the chair, pulling her legs tight to her chest. Finally Chrissy gave in, resting her head on her knees and letting the feelings pour out of her body.

She wasn't sure how long it took for the emotions to work their way through her system, but when she could finally breathe again, she felt achy and drained. A rustle drew her attention and she looked up to see Landen, clad only in his jeans, leaning against the house, watching her closely.

Chrissy buried her head in her knees, knowing that her crying had been neither short, nor particularly graceful. She could feel her eyes were puffy and she was certain her face was blotchy and tearstained. "Please, just go away," she muttered when his hand fell across her shoulder.

"Chrissy, you know I can't do that." His voice was full of compassion and concern. It would make her cry further, if she had any tears left.

He moved in front of her, pulling her arms away from her knees with a light tug. Without the support, her body uncurled and she found herself looking down into Landen's eyes. His bent knees were flush with hers, his firm hands grasping her sore legs at the thighs.

"Tell me what's wrong." Pure resolve was etched on his beautiful features.

She'd seen him look this way at the station when she dropped off files. The detective bent over his desk, ignoring everything else as he worked a case like a puzzle, worrying away at problems meticulously until everything clicked into place. Even Cavanaugh begrudgingly admitted to Chrissy that Landen deserved his reputation as a case closer. He'd walk through witness statements again and again until new evidence came to light. As surly as he could be with coworkers, he had the unique gift of making people feel secure enough to open up. Chrissy knew he wouldn't leave without answers.

"What's wrong?" she parroted, trying to figure out how to tell him the truth. Finally, it burst forth. "You. Me. This whole thing. It's all wrong."

Landen bolted up, taking a few strides away from the chair. His breathing increased, making his bare shoulders heave. Seeing his hands clench, Chrissy knew she had made him angry. Part of her hoped he'd yell, that he'd revert to the sarcastic jerk he said he'd been before instead of the affectionate wolf he'd been this weekend, the one who was her mate. Maybe that would make it easier when he left.

"It is?" His voice came out gravely and he didn't turn. Somehow this quiet acceptance made it worse. "And why is that?"

"Because you have no reason to stay, and when I tell you what I know, you won't want
to."

Landen turned, watching Chrissy intensely as she continued to babble.

"I knew you were a wolf the second I saw you. All the signs were there—your quick reactions, your changing eyes. But I know all the packs around here, and you didn't smell like any of them. When I watched more closely I saw how agitated you got just before the shift, and I realized that you weren't taking any joy in being a wolf. The only thing that made sense was that you hadn't learned how to control it. You never mentioned family, so I figured maybe you weren't raised around wolves and you'd been fighting this part of yourself your entire life. I knew I could help you, but I didn't know why I wanted to. Now I know it's because we're connected. Landen, you're my mate."

He blinked, obviously not expecting this line of conversation.

"As a Turn, you can't begin to understand what that means. But I was told my whole life what it was to find your mate. I watched my mom and dad live it. I even thought I had it once, but it ended so badly that I was certain as a Skip, I would never find it. Mom always told me I couldn't base everything on one failed relationship. She swore I would meet the one who would complete me, but I didn't know she was going to spend the last moments of her life turning him."

"The woman who scratched me was your mother?" he questioned. The detective moved toward her, but she couldn't stop. She rose from her chair to meet his onslaught, anger at the situation filling the void left by her tears. He wanted the truth and he was going to hear it.

"Your accident happened at the sight of the crash that killed my parents. The bodies weren't marked because they must have been conscious. Their bodies were trying to heal themselves before they died. I don't know why, but my mother is the reason you are what you are." Chrissy issued a bitter laugh in Landen's face.

"What else do you know about that night?" he demanded, his hands pressing around her shoulders, his eyes searching her face. She expected confusion, but the fear she sensed in his voice cut her to the core.

"Nothing," she spit back. "I've told you; I didn't know when I came here that night that you were turned. I never expected you to claim me the way you did and until yesterday I didn't think I'd ever find a mate. You thought you could keep me away. I thought this was a simple infatuation. Now, we both know better. I'm your mate and my family turned you. Tomorrow you'll be back to Detective Sutherlund. I'll go back to that girl from Records you like to ignore and it's going to kill me. But until then, I have one more day to teach you to survive without me."

Landen's jaw clenched and his eyes narrowed. Without warning, he scooped her up and threw her over his shoulder, walking back into the house. Chrissy pounded on his back and kicked her feet, anger being the only emotion left her body was willing to recognize. He made her tell him. He couldn't leave well enough alone and now things could never be the same. How dare he make her feel this love and then ruin everything!

Landen didn't let go until he reached the bedroom where he tossed her down on the bed. Chrissy was too shocked to move. Before she realized it, his handcuffs slapped around her ankle, chaining her to the bedpost.

"What the fuck, Landen!" she screamed, yanking on the cuffs. "Exactly!" He yelled back. "What the fuck!"

His anger didn't cool hers, but it did make Chrissy pause.

"What have I done? Tell me," he demanded, running his hands through his hair distractedly before placing them on his hips. "You save me from living in hell, teach me how to embrace what I am, make love to me repeatedly, and expect me to leave you for something you had no control over? You really think so little of me?"

Chrissy's jaw dropped. Her anger fizzled momentarily then flared. "Think so little of you? I think the world of you, you bastard. For God's sake, I just admitted you're my mate. You're the one who's locked me to the bed! Not quite so perfect now that you know my family caused your change, am I?" Landen started to respond, but Chrissy cut him off viciously. "Don't lie to me! I heard the fear in your voice and you've just made sure I can't fight back. Now that you know the truth, you don't want me anymore."

Landen pinched the bridge of his nose and his face flushed red. Chrissy wished she could read his thoughts instead of waiting for him.

When he finally spoke, his words sounded carefully planned. "I told you I've wanted you for months, but I knew I wasn't good enough for you. I've done everything I could the past two days to prove to you I can be better for you. Do you understand that being turned was a punishment I fully deserved? Becoming a wolf was completely my fault. What could have possibly made you think I would blame you for the actions of your dying mother?"

Chrissy realized how seriously she had misjudged this man. All the pieces of him she had grown to love the past several months, his intelligence and compassion, she'd just ignored them and let her secret overwhelm her.

Still, something he said ate at her. "What do you mean it was a punishment? Why do you think it was your fault?"

He grabbed a shirt from the floor and slipped it on. "Because it was," he growled. "Why? Lan? What did you do?"

"Chrissy," he whispered, his eyes boring into hers. "You are inside me. We are mates. I am nothing if not yours."

Every fiber of her being felt the honesty ringing through his statement, but she noticed he didn't answer the question. "Lan, I—" she began, but was immediately silenced as he leaned over her and seized her mouth in a ravenous kiss.

When he finally broke away, he stared at her intently. "There are things I need to tell you, but I can't do this right now," he said, starting to walk away.

"Landen!" she cried, jerking against the handcuffs.

A look from him stilled her. His gaze moved to the bedside table, and Chrissy noticed her cell phone easily within reach. Did he think she was worried about her own safety? Even handcuffed, she trusted her mate more than anyone else. A phone wouldn't help if she didn't know where he was. The wolf was not yet gone and right now it looked as if he could gnaw his own arm off. She couldn't stand it if he hurt himself because of her. Once more she rattled the handcuffs and Landen held up the key.

"Can I trust you not to leave?" he asked.

"Can I trust you not to hurt yourself?" she responded eying him levelly. When he nodded she continued. "You can leave them on if you're really that worried about me leaving."

"I'm going for a walk." Landen slid the key next to her phone, but left the cuffs on her ankle. "I need to clear my head and you need some rest. I know you didn't sleep last night."

Chrissy recognized the gesture of trust. "Promise me you'll come back," she pleaded, still worried for his safety.

He merely kissed her forehead and stalked out the door. Her mind raced. Landen was mad because he cared. He'd referred to her as his mate. Even after learning that his suffering was due to her parents, he still wanted her. Upsetting as all of this was, his words filled her with hope.

Briefly, she pondered how to fix the situation, and decided they'd have to figure it out together. Chrissy knew Landen was right. She had to sleep so she'd be able to discuss everything logically.

Examining her ankle, she found Landen had been incredibly thoughtful in subduing her. The cuffs were slightly loose and it was easy to find a comfortable position that didn't make them chafe her skin. With that problem solved, she could handle anything else when he returned. Chrissy yawned and within minutes fell into an exhausted sleep.

Chapter Ten

Several hours later Chrissy was awakened by a soft click and a large hand gently encircling her ankle. Drowsily, she looked up to see Landen beside the bed in a chair he'd dragged in from the kitchen. She wondered how long he'd been sitting there. His hair was unruly. His eyes were stormy. Worry was laced through his tight shoulders and he refused to look up from where his thumb was delicately rubbing away the red imprint left on her skin by the handcuffs.

"Why don't you get cleaned up and I'll bring in something to eat. We need to talk." Chrissy reached out to put a comforting hand on Landen's arm, but he stood and walked

out of the bedroom, closing the door behind him. Her stomach dropped. Until this got resolved she wasn't going to be able to eat anything. Still, she did what he suggested and headed into the bathroom.

Splashing some water on her face, Chrissy tried to clear her head. That feeling of dread was back, settled like a brick in her stomach. His quiet manner made her uncertain that Landen's affection would cause him to stay. Pushing down her emotions, Chrissy brushed her teeth and ran a comb through her tangled hair before deciding it was a lost cause and threw it in a loose braid. She didn't bother to shower or change.

When she returned she found some venison chili and fruit sitting on a small table by the windows. Her thumb traced the side of the bowl as she dropped heavily into the oversized reading chair that occupied this side of the room. Landen walked in a minute later with a cup of tea for her and a bottle of beer for himself.

Chrissy took a sip of the steaming beverage as Landen pulled the kitchen chair in front of her and straddled it, effectively blocking any type of escape. He didn't need to bother. She watched his nimble fingers twitch against the wooden back of the chair as he contemplated what to say.

He took a couple pulls from the bottle before he finally issued a sigh. "Tell me what it means to be mated."

It wasn't not exactly what Chrissy expected, but it was a place to start. "I've never had to explain this before," she began uncomfortably.

"Try," he urged.

"Okay. It's not the same for everybody. For full Weres there's something rooted in their DNA. When they meet, there's this instant attraction but it's not just normal chemistry. It's instinctive, a soul connection that never fades. Their mate is able to balance the wolf and the human in them, making them completely, independently themselves, but at the same time a connected unit. They become so completely entwined with one another that..." she paused, sighing.

"Mom used to say it was like feeling two heartbeats in your chest and knowing that both belong to you. It's such a strong biological reaction that ignoring it can make a Were physically ill. They can't fight it. They don't want to. There is no question of ever being apart."

Landen listened intently. His thumb thumped along the top of the chair and he nodded in understanding. Chrissy thought he was taking the information fairly well. It was something awkward to explain, and she knew that next she would have to tell him how in this, as in all things wolf, she was slightly defective.

Uncomfortably, she shifted in her chair, took a deep breath, and continued. "For Skips, it's not quite as easy. The wolf runs through our veins, but it's not properly expressed." She gave him a wry smile, feeling the painful truth in the pit of her stomach. "Like I said earlier, everything but the shifting. It complicates things. We feel the pull just as intensely, we get sick just as easily, but we can't sense the reciprocation. I never understood the hell in that before, but it's what I feel with you. There's an ache in my chest like I've been holding my breath forever and only you can give me permission to exhale."

Landen looked a little dazed by that information. Chrissy tried to give him a few moments to process. She concentrated on his fingers raking through his hair instead of the oppressive silence. When she thought she couldn't bare it a second longer, he spoke.

"So, this morning when you said going back to the way things were before would kill you..." His eyes searched her face intently.

"I meant it." It was getting to hard to look at him, so Chrissy ducked her head and curled into a ball around herself. Two days ago she knew this weekend would be difficult but it had spun out of her control. She was more exposed now than she'd ever been. But she wouldn't have given up these past few days for anything. She held her breath, wondering how he would react.

Landen took a long draw of his beer. "When did you know?"

"Yesterday," she admitted. "Something happened inside me when you demanded my submission in the shower, and it deepened on the hill when you asked me to make you mine. But it didn't take root until the cabin. I never should have demanded you claim me so close to transition on the night of the full moon. I didn't think about what it might mean. I've never needed to before. Then at the lake I thought about Monday morning and it just hurt so bad."

Chrissy knew she sounded miserable, but she wasn't ready for Landen's look of surprise. Her hand shot out to grab his. This was going to end poorly, yet still she needed to make it okay for him. The words spilled out."You don't have to worry, though. Turns have a choice in mating. It's the one good thing about being a Turn. The wolf isn't ingrained; it's layered on top of your humanity. So you have the strength to deny the connection without it physically hurting you." Landen pushed away from his chair and paced. A look of disgust crossed his face, wounding her in ways she wasn't ready to admit. Chrissy kept babbling, staring at her hands, trying to ignore the pain in her chest. "You know this is a safe place to come when you're going to shift. I've taught you enough that you don't have to take the tranquilizers anymore. I can keep my distance if that's what you need. I'll stay at the cabin. You never have to see me. I'm sure Cavanaugh will help me put in for a transfer to Escanaba PD." Chrissy stopped. The thought of having Landen in this house without her, so close and yet completely inaccessible, was hellish. She struggled to catch her breath.

"What are you talking about?" he asked.

Looking up, she noticed that he'd stopped in front of her, his face frozen in horror. Landen dropped to his knees by the edge of her chair. "You still think I could leave you?" His right hand tenderly cupped Chrissy's face as his eyes searched hers. His voice was quiet, pained. "Chrissy, Turns may have a choice, but I don't. I've loved you for every second of these last six months. Whatever happened between us, I'm glad you finally feel it too."

Her heart swelled as she gaped at him—this perfect man, her mate.

Leaning in, he pulled her into a passionate kiss. The hunger in his lips was obvious, yet restrained. When he pulled back, he rested his forehead against hers. "You've been inside me since the moment you first walked into Homicide. It drove me crazy, not knowing what this was. I
I could smell you wherever you were in the building, could hear your breathing before you walked in the room. To say I could feel your heartbeat is a gross understatement. Your heartbeat was my own."

There was no need to question his sincerity. Landen's eyes yearned for her acceptance.

His body radiated the earthy musk that Chrissy had come to know so intimately. How could he have handled this for that long?

"Six months? That had to have been torture. Landen, why didn't you say something?" He nodded, his shoulders slumped in misery. She wondered how he could be upset when

he now knew she loved him too. Landen issued a deep sigh.

"I felt you when I was here too. I figured it was proof I'd lost my mind. Even here I couldn't escape you. Now, I know you must have been at the cabin, freeing your wolf even though you don't change," Landen paused, as if contemplating his next words. "That connection, can it ever go away?"

Chrissy shook her head. "It's what causes the sickness," she whispered. Landen finished off his bottle of beer and set it on the table. She could tell he was steeling himself to tell her something so she waited, giving him the time he needed.

"I'm so sorry, love. At the office I kept my distance because I didn't want to hurt you, but once you were here, once I knew you understood what I was, I couldn't help myself. You were just trying to help me, and I couldn't keep my damn hands off you. You're tied to me for life and in a minute you won't be able to stand the sight of me."

She looked at him, confused. "Chrissy, I killed your parents."

Chapter Eleven

All the air left her lungs at once. It wasn't possible. How could Landen have anything to do with her parents' death? It was unthinkable. The emotional roller coaster she'd been on this morning was giving her an intense headache, and she shook her head back and forth trying to process what he'd said. When she didn't speak for several minutes, Landen reached to caress her face. Something snapped.

"Why would you say something so cruel?" She smacked at his hand, her voice trembling in anger. "You want me to leave? You want me to hate you? Why?" Her voice was growing progressively louder. "Why stay with me the last few days? Why tell me you love me and then throw such a horrible lie in my face? My parents died in a car accident!"

By this point Chrissy was screaming. She realized she'd stood at some point and was in front of Landen with her finger pressed into his chest, but she had no recollection of getting up. Landen held her wrists carefully.

"It's not a lie. I've carried around the guilt for that night for nearly two years. I didn't know they were your parents until this morning. I," he paused. "I don't know how to explain."

"Well figure it out," she hissed, wrenching herself away from his grip. She stalked over to the backpack on the floor, yanking out a pair of jeans. Turning away from him, she put them on roughly.

"Chrissy, what are you doing?" His voice crossed the line between concerned and panicked.

"I'm getting dressed, goddammit!" she yelled, pulling the keys off the bedside table and flinging them at him. Landen flinched at the impact, but caught them as they hit his chest. "You're responsible for my parents' death? You have a whole car ride to tell me why. Now, take me to the crash site."

She didn't look at him as she stomped past him and out to his SUV. Ripping open the door, she threw herself into the passenger seat and crossed her arms, leaving her anger on a slow burn. Landen simply started the vehicle and pulled out onto the access road. It'd take them a good forty-five minutes to reach the site, but she refused to talk to him. About fifteen minutes went by before he spoke.

"Your heart rate's almost back to normal. Do you want to talk now?"

She kept her mouth shut and her eyes on the trees as they raced by out the window.

"All right, I'll talk. You know how I told you that you wouldn't have liked me before? It's true. I was so arrogant. I'd graduated top marks at the academy, was the youngest person to be promoted to detective, and I had no shortage of women wanting to date me. I was good and I knew it. I'd been dating this girl, Jes, a few weeks. Nothing serious. I didn't even like her that much, truth be told, but she was hot, which was all that mattered to me at the time."

Chrissy rolled her eyes at the window. He couldn't possibly have seen it, but Landen chuckled humorlessly.

"I told you, you would've looked right through me. So, Mark and I had just gotten off shift and decided to go to this new restaurant to check the bar and the waitresses. In walks Jes with her ex. I should have let it be, but I'd had a few by that point and I went nuts, started screaming and making a huge scene. Her ex was a worthless asshole, must have been a pattern of hers to date scumbags. He didn't even try to defend her, but the guy in line behind them, I guess he was your dad, he stepped up to put me in my place."

Tears rimmed the corners of Chrissy's eyes. Her dad would never let any woman be insulted when he was around. If there was any sort of altercation, of course he would have stepped in to mediate.

"He was a big guy with salt and pepper hair. I had a chip on my shoulder and figured I'd take him no problem, so I took a swing. He blocked it. It pissed me off, so I took another one but I was off balance. I basically ran myself right into the guy's fist. Mark decided to help me out by telling your dad he could be arrested for assaulting an officer. Your mom just kept saying it wasn't worth it. When she finally pulled him out of the restaurant, he was apologizing, saying they'd celebrate another night."

"It was their anniversary dinner," Chrissy whispered, nodding.

"Shit," Landen cursed, finally reaching the junction to 29 and turning north.

Chrissy shuddered. She hadn't traveled this road since before the accident. In her anger this had seemed like a good idea, but the knot in her stomach made her question that now.

"So a few hours later Mark's calmed me down and sobered me up. Then I get a message from Bridgette. We've been called in to investigate a site that Traffic found. I bitched the whole way there about Traffic being so lazy that we had to take their case. One look at the site shut me right up. The car had rolled so many times that nobody could figure out why the bodies were so clean. They thought it was a body dump. There was blood everywhere on this couple, but not a scratch on them. And then I recognized them from the restaurant."

A sob escaped Chrissy's throat. They had to have been conscious. Their bodies had gone into a semi-hibernation state to perform the intense super-healing that would have been necessary to combat such serious wounds. The damage itself must have been excruciating, the healing even worse, as the bones and tissues tried to knit themselves together one hundred times faster than natural. It wasn't enough to save them, and yet they would have been aware of every bit of pain.

"God, Chrissy. I'm so sorry I have to tell you this." His hand raked through his curls. She could tell he wanted to reach out, to comfort her, but was hesitant since he was the one causing the pain.

"I went down to examine the bodies. They wouldn't have been on the road if I hadn't fought with your dad in the restaurant. They would have been happily enjoying their anniversary in a restaurant instead of here on this road. I needed to look at what I'd done, face that I'd caused this so it would never happen again. That's when your mom scratched me." Landen pulled off to the side of the road and nodded. "We're here."

Carefully, Chrissy removed herself from the car and crept her way down the small hillside. She heard a car door slam behind her, but ignored it, too intent on what she saw. Several small bouquets of flowers had been laid in the ditch. Landen stepped up behind her and handed her a fresh arrangement of brightly colored flowers that he'd obviously purchased the day before while they were in town.

"I didn't know where they were buried, or if they'd be remembered, so I remember. "I bring a new set every month on my way back to Marquette."

Chrissy smiled sadly. This man, her perfect brooding detective, had honored her parents' memory all this time, even when she couldn't. He'd kept the guilt for something that wasn't truly his fault and suffered through shifting as a punishment, not knowing the joy that could come with being a wolf.

If he'd known her mom, Landen would have understood that what he'd seen as a curse had been meant as a gift. With her final breath, Chrissy's mom had seen him and forgiven.

She brought the flowers to her nose, smelling the light fragrance as she stepped back into Landen's warm chest. She pulled his arms around her and felt him dip his head into her shoulder. His whole body both supported and sagged against hers. She tossed the flowers to the forest floor.

"I miss you, Mom and Dad," she whispered. "I miss you so much. But I want you to know I've found my mate, and he's everything you always told me he'd be." Landen stiffened then pulled her closer. "I love him, and I know he's going to take care of me. Your little ghost is going to be just fine."

Landen's head pulled away from her. She could feel his hands shaking as he turned her toward him.

"What did you just say?" His face was colorless.

"It was my nickname, like on the wine bottle. Mom and Dad always called me their 'little ghost wolf.'"

For a minute he stared at her, then glanced at the flowers before wrapping her in a hug and spinning her around, laughing.

"It's not a curse," he said, his voice filled with wonder. "It was meant to happen." "Landen, what are you..." His blue eyes sparkled brighter than Chrissy had ever seen

them before. Her heart lifted seeing the weight that had suddenly removed itself from his shoulders.

"'Take care. My ghost.' It's what your mother said when she scratched me. All this time I thought she meant she'd haunt me, but she wanted me to find you. She turned me so I could be your mate."

Landen grasped Chrissy's hand, leading her up the hill. "Before I thought I'd hurt you, so I kept my distance. But now I know better. I don't intend to ever let you go." He pulled her up the last few steps and into his strong embrace. Leaning down, he kissed her, exploring her mouth with his until they were both breathless. "I am your mate and you are mine. We were created for each other and nothing will convince me differently."

"Lan," she breathed, wrapping her arms around his neck.

Moments later, they were in the SUV headed back to the lake house. Chrissy felt a sense of peace she hadn't in a long time. She rolled down the windows let the pine-scented air fill the car. Route 29 was no longer intimidating.

All too soon Landen eased the car off onto a side road used for snowmobiling in the winter. Chrissy was about to ask what he was doing when his earthy, feral scent washed over her. Looking over, she saw a roguish grin on the detective's face.

"We've been through quite a bit today, haven't we, love?"

Remembering their interrupted fun in the store the previous day, Chrissy nodded, batting her eyelashes and giving him a come hither look. "It was awful kind of you to pick me up off the side of the road like that, Detective Sutherlund. I hope you'll let me repay your kindness." Her hand drifted up over his leg and brushed the bulge starting in his pants.

"What exactly did you have in mind?"

Chrissy bit her lip coyly and unbuckled her seatbelt. Her hand began to massage the front of his low-slung jeans. "Well, Detective, there's something I'd love to do, but I'm afraid you might arrest me for lewd conduct."

"Oh," was all he said as he cocked an eyebrow, but Chrissy could see him swell in anticipation. She leaned across the center console of the car, happy his SUV had so much space, and unbuttoned his jeans. His semi-hard cock tented his boxers and Chrissy cooed, rubbing gently through the fabric.

"I've never gone down on a guy in a car before," she murmured. "Such a tight, confined space, the chance that we could get caught if someone drove by. Would you let me taste you, Detective?" Chrissy glanced up through her eyelashes.

Landen licked his lips, letting her know he was enjoying her description immensely. "You are a surprisingly dirty girl, Ms. Lorcan," he mock- scolded as she removed him from his shorts. He was swollen and glistening. Chrissy flicked her tongue out and licked the tip, causing Landen's head to dip back and a groan to escape.

Her mouth watered at the salty taste of him and the feral smell flooded the car as his desire increased. It was not all games. Chrissy ached to connect with her mate after the turmoil of the last twelve hours, and Landen felt right in her hand

and on her tongue. She lowered her mouth onto his cock, taking long, slow pulls as she twirled her tongue around the head, causing him to gasp.

"God, Chrissy. I love your mouth," Landen cried, griping the back of her head to bring her closer. It was all the encouragement she needed. Chrissy gripped her hand around the base of his shaft, widening her jaw to take him deeper.

Her tongue pulled languidly along the underside of his cock, lapping at the veins and tender skin as she pumped. Plunging down again she sheathed him with her mouth. When Landen issued another cry, Chrissy began to suck faster, increasing the intensity of her pulls. He bucked against her lips.

The tension in his body was beautiful, the intimacy between them electrifying. Chrissy relished the fact that she could bring him, the man she loved, the one made to be her mate, undone with her tongue. She could feel his climax approaching and she moaned around his cock.

"Fucking hell!" he cursed through gritted teeth.

Chrissy pulled her head away and slid her lips off him with an audible pop. She looked up questioningly, then heard the unmistakable click of a car door opening behind them. Glancing through the back window, Chrissy cringed when she noticed the car had the distinctive markings of a police vehicle.

"Keep down. I'll take care of this," Landen hissed, trying to shove himself back into his pants. It was no easy task with how she had been working him. Still Landen managed to get himself together and step out of the car before the officer made it down the path.

"Landen? Thought that looked like your car," she heard a deep male voice.

"Jesus, Mark." Landen leaned one hand on his hip and ran the other through his hair. Relief was evident in his tone. "You have no idea how glad I am it's you."

Chrissy watched a stocky Vietnamese man built like a linebacker grab her mate's hand and slap him on the back.

"You having car trouble, man? I was headed to Iron Mountain to help my brother-in-law fix the roof. I'll give you a ride."

"Thanks, Mark. The car's fine. I just pulled off to clear my head."

Landen really was an awful liar. Chrissy heard the catch in his voice and she could tell from the look on Mark's face that he did too. She'd been in Traffic often enough, but she'd never met Landen's friend before. Apparently now was the time. Chrissy delicately wiped her lips, ran her fingers thorough her hair, and hopped out of the car. Mark eyed her curiously as she walked over.

"Didn't realize you had someone with you," he said, shooting a confused look at Landen. Chrissy ignored her mate's sigh and stretched out a hand that Mark took.

"Hi Mark, I'm Chrissy. Nice to finally know you're not just Landen's excuse to ignore me."

"Wait. You're Chrissy? Like *the* Chrissy? Chrissy from Records, Chrissy?" The traffic cop barely kept his jaw closed as his attention shifted from her to Landen.

Instantly, Chrissy found herself wrapped in the burly man's arms. She giggled as her feet lifted up off the ground.

"So much for keeping a low profile at work," Landen chuckled.

Mark gently set Chrissy back down. "How'd you finally get up the balls?" he asked Landen and then blushed as if realizing Chrissy was still there.

She smiled and slipped a hand in the back pocket of Landen's jeans.

"Sorry, it's just that this idiot has been putting off asking you out for months, and now here you are and..." Mark trailed off, looking between the two. When his eyes fell on Landen's jeans he finally realized what was going on. "And I'm a fucking idiot," Mark acknowledged, enunciating each word painfully and rubbing his forehead with a grimace. "Right."

"Mark, I'd really appreciate it if you didn't say anything at the office," Landen said as he griped Chrissy's shoulder affectionately. "At least until we get some things figured out first."

"Got it," the officer replied, heading back to his car. "But get back on the road, okay. I passed County not far back and that asshole hates city cops. It'd make his day to haul you in on public indecency."

As the car pulled away Landen leaned down to kiss the top of Chrissy's head. She snuggled into his side as they strolled back toward his SUV.

"Much as I was enjoying your repayment," Landen said. "I don't think either of us actually wants to get arrested today."

"The only person I'm letting handcuff me is you," Chrissy agreed, buckling herself into the passenger seat. "Besides it's getting late anyway. I want to make you a nice dinner before we go running. I promise to make it up to you later, but for now let's go home."

"Home." Landen smiled. "I like the sound of that."

Chapter Twelve

Chrissy was never going to tire of waking to Landen's body twined around her. It felt right. There was no other way to explain how perfectly their bodies fit together. She placed a kiss to his curls and ran her hand along his shoulder thoughtfully.

What was it like for people who didn't know this joy? As a Skip she may never feel the reciprocation of Landen's love like she would if she were a full Were, but never again would she doubt his devotion. He showed it to her every second they were together.

The man in him sought out her playfulness and intelligence, enjoying the way she kept him on his toes. The wolf valued her strength and passion, protecting her fiercely while acknowledging she was an Alpha in her own right.

They'd barely gotten home in time for dinner last night. After a quick shower, Chrissy had grilled venison steaks and served them to Landen in nothing but a chef's apron. She was glad she'd thought to put the oven on warm because her attire had made him take her right there on the kitchen counter. Dinner would have been cold by the time they'd gotten to it.

After the steaks, they'd taken a short walk by the cliffs to stretch before their run. When he'd shifted, Landen had knocked her down, rolling over her and rubbing every piece of skin with his tawny muzzle to fully scent their bodies. Every animal in the forest had known they belonged to each other.

She breathed into his hair, enjoying the woodsy smell that was her mate, wishing they could stay in the lake house forever. Chrissy could tell by the change in his breathing that Landen was waking up. He nuzzled closer to her. For several moments, Chrissy traced invisible patterns on his back with her fingertips until he rolled and pulled her to his chest.

"I suppose we need to talk about how we're going to handle this."

"Mm," she agreed, enjoying her new pillow. "Sleeping with the landlord will get you significant discounts on your weekend rentals."

He laughed and trailed a finger down her cheek. "Things shouldn't be too bad at work since we're not in the same department. We'll notify our supervisors. Bridge is going to give me hell for not doing this sooner."

"Cavanaugh will give you hell for doing this period," Chrissy murmured.

"Give me hell," he questioned. "Why not you?" Landen's hand was drifting across her arms and side, tickling lightly, but it wasn't why Chrissy giggled.

"Because he likes me. If I recall correctly he was calling you the hind end of a horse last time the two of you were in a room together."

"True," Landen conceded, raising his eyebrows. "I'm going to start looking for a house this week."

"A house?"

"I'm not living away from you a second longer than I have to," he growled. "The lease is up on my apartment. We can find someplace for the two of us. Someplace just outside town with some extra space and a yard for the kids."

"Kids?" Chrissy whispered, raising her head to look at him.

Landen, leaned in, kissing her gently. "When you're ready, love. I expect to give you a whole pack of little wolflings." Landen moved, hovering over her with a wicked grin. "Or die trying."

Chrissy peeked up at her mate. Her body quickening as her chest swelled with love. A tear of joy slipped from her eye and Landen brushed it away with his thumb. Her hand reached down to stroke him and found him already hard for her.

"Lan," she breathed. "My mate. Make love to me."

The crush of his body atop hers was breathtaking. Chrissy's arms threaded around his shoulders, and her legs wrapped his waist. No part of her was disconnected from him. As his fingers probed her entrance, she ran kisses up and down his neck. Her body was attuned to his touch, already primed for the sensual pleasure his hands provided as they slid in and out, preparing her for his length.

Landen was attentive, listening to each small sound Chrissy emitted, waiting until they reached a fevered pitch before removing his fingers. With ease, he lined himself up and entered her with his swollen cock. A deep moan rumbled in his chest as he sank down, sheathing himself completely in her wet folds. Chrissy could feel the press of him against her cervix, shooting a tingle through her with every tiny movement.

She rocked her hips up gently, every motion causing shudders of pleasure to ripple through her body and gasps to escape Landen's lips. He pulled himself up, giving his hips greater leverage and Chrissy used the change to swirl her tongue around his nipple. The tenderness caused Landen to buck, pinning her hips to the bed with his before pulling back sharply.

"Fuck," he exhaled, as lost in the moment as she.

Chrissy took control, thrusting her hips up underneath him so he pierced her with fierce strokes which offered indescribably wonderful sensations. That familiar heat was coiling in her belly. Her head was light, making it hard to concentrate, but Landen breathed into her ear, his words cutting through the haze.

"I love you, Chrissy."

One more thrust and Chrissy came undone in his arms, tears spilling down her cheeks from the intensity. She gripped Landen tightly as she spasmed, pulling his body down, needing to feel the press of her mate on top of her. Landen rolled his hips, drawing out her orgasm, and then offered a strong thrust that pushed her straight into another.

His movements didn't abate. Orgasm after orgasm rolled through Chrissy, draining her body, until finally Landen grunted and exploded inside her. Their mingled passion spilled onto her thigh when he finally removed himself from her.

Landen pushed up, pressing his forehead to hers as he stared into Chrissy's eyes. "You are mine and I am yours. We are mates, and I will spend the rest of my life proving myself worthy of the title."

Acknowledgments

My sincere gratitude to the many people who helped me bring Landen and Chrissy to life. I would like to thank the fabulous **Torrance Sené** (Teresa Conner): friend, editor, promoter, and cover designer. Without your many talents, this book would never have come to fruition. I appreciate your inspirational words more than you know. My everlasting thanks to **Daniel**, for your love and support. It isn't easy to deal with a writer's lifestyle, and you never complain about all the time I spend scribbling. Thanks to my original readers **Aletheia, Connie, Elena, Hailey** , and **Renee** and my beta readers **Karen, Orey, Amy**, and **Allison**. Your opinions and generous comments were much appreciated and kept me excited about writing a better story. Finally, thank YOU...my readers. May this book be as wonderful a journey for you as it was for me.

About the Author

Harley Easton is a Renaissance woman dabbling in everything life offers. She's worked at a major theme park, found expert witnesses for legal cases, and been a guest lecturer at a well-known national museum. Putting experience and insanity to good use, she's become an author specializing in erotic fiction. See what inspires Harley and get erotic writing advice on her blog.

Find Harley online:

Facebook: http://facebook.com/harleyeastonauthor
Twitter: https://twitter.com/Harley_Easton
GoodReads:
https://www.goodreads.com/author/show/8506548.Harley_Easton
Visit my website: http://www.harleyeaston.com